M   Forrest, Richard
      Death under the lilacs

APR 25 '85	DATE DUE		
APR 26 '86	SEP 17 '85	APR 4 '86	AG 5 '94
MAY 3 '85	SEP 25 '85	JUN 26 '86	SE 20 '95
MAY 11 '85	OCT 2 '85	APR 12 '86	NO 07 '95
MAY 28 '85	OCT 24 '85	NOV 10 '88	
JUN 5 '85	NOV 15 '85	NOV 25 '88	
JUN 17 '85	NOV 26 '85	MY 12 '90	
JUN 25 '85	DEC 11 '85	OC 2 '90	
JUL 5 '85	JAN 2 '85	OC 12 '92	
JUL 27 '85	JAN 24 '86	OC 24 '92	
AUG 20 '85	JAN 31 '86	OC 29 '92	
AUG 28 '85	FEB 17 '86	NO 18 '92	
GAYLORD 234	MAR 27 '86	NO 25 '92	PRINTED IN U.S.A. DEMCO

Death
Under
the
Lilacs

Death
Under
the
Lilacs

Richard Forrest

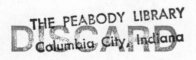
St. Martin's Press
New York

Design by M. Paul

Library of Congress Cataloging in Publication Data

Forrest, Richard, 1932-
  ⚶ Death under the lilacs.
    I. Title.
PS3556.0739D5   1985   813'.54   84-22886
ISBN 0-312-18878-1

First Edition

10 9 8 7 6 5 4 3 2 1

For Bo

. . . who toiled . . .

*Death
Under
the
Lilacs*

1

HE DECIDED NOT TO rape her.

It might be interesting to force himself upon her and watch her humiliation and degradation, but that wasn't part of the plan. He couldn't help but be attracted to her. She exuded a sexuality in the simplest of her movements that he found disconcerting. Erotic images kept recurring, but he forced the thoughts back into the tight mental compartments where they belonged.

The days of following her every movement had forced her into his dreams, and that hadn't been in the plan either. There would be time. If he changed his mind later, there would always be the opportunity to do with her what he wanted.

But this had to be done tonight.

The plans were complete. Necessary peripheral events had been set in motion, and the whole complex was building up an internal velocity that would fly out of control unless he proceeded with its final execution.

Yes, it had to be tonight.

The location was not of his choosing, but dictated by her personal habits. He had followed her carefully for three weeks, charting her moves and timing her actions with a stopwatch clenched in a damp fist until he had reached a point where he could accurately predict nearly every movement of her day.

As with most people, her actions fell into a predictable pattern.

It couldn't be done at her home. Although the house was located on an isolated tract of land wooded on three sides, with the fourth overlooking the Connecticut River, there were inherent risks. He had observed the house through binoculars, but had never actually been inside, and he knew from experience that people who lived in rural areas often had various weapons close at hand. Then there was her husband, who seemed to be constantly at her side while she was home.

Her weekdays were spent at the State Capitol, where she was never alone. Her activities at the Capitol were at a frenzied pace: senate sessions, committee meetings, or a party caucus that surrounded her with fellow legislators, lobbyists, or constituents.

He had briefly considered making the attempt on an isolated stretch of road. It would be possible to force her car off the highway onto the shoulder and continue from there. He had discarded that possibility after calculating the probability of passing motorists who might come to her aid or later identify his van.

It was logical that it be done at the shopping center where she stopped every Thursday evening from seven until nine.

The Murphysville, Connecticut, shopping mall was located on the outskirts of town. It was anchored on one end by a Stop and Shop supermarket and on the far side by a branch of Caldor's discount house. The interior of the leg of the center was occupied by a pharmacy, liquor store, and bookstore.

Bea Wentworth followed the same pattern each Thursday evening. She parked her car at seven, then spent ten minutes browsing in the bookstore and half an hour in the discount store. She finished by doing a week's grocery shopping at the supermarket. She pushed her grocery cart to the small station wagon and loaded her items through the tailgate, after which she drove briskly back to Nutmeg Hill, arriving around nine o'clock.

2

On the first night he followed her, he had gone into the bookstore knowing that he could safely browse without appearing conspicuous.

He had fled the store when he had come upon the large display of Wentworth children's books. A man-size cutout of a Wobbly monster had stared at him with red accusing eyes. A dozen of Lyon Wentworth's childrens' books with gaily colored dust jackets were clutched in the creature's paws.

He had left the store hurriedly and huddled in the shadows of a nearby phone booth.

Tonight she had parked two dozen feet from the nearest light pole. Her car was partially in the shadows and he had been lucky enough to find a space two removed where he could park the van.

He would do it while she fumbled with her keys to unlock the tailgate.

He watched Bea enter the supermarket and then returned to his van. He had promised himself a cigarette, and stripped the cellophane off a new package and slowly extracted one. He tapped it methodically against the steering wheel, ceremoniously lit it, and leaned back against the headrest to savor the mellow glow of anticipation.

Lyon Wentworth sighed. The Wobblies were gone.

They had retreated to some dark, secret place where they now rested with limpid eyes and slowly thumping tails. They were quiet, nearly comatose, and he barely felt their vitality. They had been missing for several days now and he needed them. They would not speak or let their presence be known in any manner, and that made it impossible for him to translate their adventures onto the typewriter that sat so disapprovingly before him.

He looked out the window. Far below the parapet that surrounded the patio, the river moved sluggishly, colored in dark hues from the dying day. A bleak gray sky pressed down on the high ridge lines, and the house sat under a teacup of low nimbus clouds.

His benign monsters were gone. He had tried to recall them by performing the ritualistic chores: He had replaced the ribbon in the typewriter and seen to it that a ream of clean yellow paper was piled neatly to his left and that gold paper clips glinted from a small cup on the right. Nothing had worked. The words wouldn't come.

He wished Bea would come home and give him the necessary excuse to leave his work, cover the typewriter, and mix drinks.

He had last seen her that morning when he found her engrossed on the kitchen phone. Her eyes had followed him as he poured coffee from the electric percolator, and she had wedged the receiver between her shoulder and ear while miming for him to pour her a cup. He had pretended not to understand until her eyebrow had arched in exasperation and he had finally given in and poured.

He had leaned against the kitchen counter with the large mug cupped between his hands and observed his wife. Bea's figure was trim and well proportioned. She spoke with an energy that seemed to possess her slight frame. Occasionally, as if to emphasize a point, her hand would ruffle the edge of her closely cropped hair.

If Lyon had been asked to identify his wife's most salient characteristic, he would have replied that it was her energy. She was a vital person, with strong opinions that she defended on the floor of the state senate and a robustness that intruded into nearly every facet of her life. He loved her very much and sometimes felt guilty that he drew so much of his own sustenance from her.

"I think, Senator, that we are in agreement," she had said in conclusion that morning as she hung up the phone.

"You're looking very political this morning," Lyon had said.

"Wingate is resigning from the state senate to run for the vacant congressional seat."

"Who will be majority leader?"

Bea smiled. "It's gonna be a tough one."

"Ramsey will oppose you."

"He always does."

"He still thinks that women should be kept barefoot and pregnant."

"About time he learned," Bea had said as she drank from her mug and smiled at him over the rim.

"This state has never had a woman majority leader."

"We're on our second woman governor."

"Objection withdrawn. I wish you luck, hon." He kissed her on the forehead and refilled her cup from the percolator. He was actually ambivalent toward her new goal. While he knew that she was a courageous politician and had chits to call upon for support, he worried that she might lose. He wanted nothing to touch his wife. He wanted no harm or pain to come her way, and he would protect her from all that he could.

She gathered her pocketbook and keys. "I'll be late tonight. I have to do the shopping."

"I can do it."

"Oh, no. It would give you an excuse for not working."

"It's just not coming."

She had kissed him. "It will. Give it a chance."

And then she was gone, and the whole day and part of the evening had stretched before him.

A thumping on the front door broke his reverie, and he almost knocked over the desk chair in his eagerness to leave the study.

Rocco Herbert was slouched against the door frame and gave Lyon a casual salute as the door opened. "Happy-hour time yet?"

"You know it!" Lyon replied and yanked his large friend inside the house. "I'll get the ice. You mix."

In the kitchen, Lyon levered ice-tray partitions and dumped loose cubes into a silver ice bucket. "Martha must be out of town," he yelled into the living room where the large police chief mixed a pitcher of martinis at a portable bar cart.

"She is," the chief replied. "Hurry up with the ice."

Lyon placed the full ice bucket on the cart, and Rocco immediately scooped up half a dozen cubes for his pitcher. Lyon poured a snifter glass half full of Dry Sack sherry. He waited for his friend to finish his drink ministrations.

Rocco carefully stirred his martini and poured himself a double. He held up his glass in a toast. "Cheers."

"Skoal," Lyon replied and both men drank.

"Martha's at her sister's for the night. I thought you and Bea might come over, and I'll throw a couple-three steaks on the fire."

"Sounds good." Lyon sipped his sherry. "It will be an improvement to an otherwise lousy day."

"Mine wasn't exactly a winner either." Rocco leaned back on the couch, his six-foot-six frame overlapping the furniture. "Do you realize that the proportion of drunken housewives is increasing arithmetically? They get a snootful and then, for reasons I do not comprehend, call my office and insist that I throw them in a cell."

"The spouses call?"

"Hell, no! The drinkees. Booze seems to bring out all the original-sin syndromes."

"I won't ask who it is. Murphysville's too small and I would probably know them."

"You do."

Rocco's gigantic proportions presided over the town's constabulary, which sometimes reached a peak force of twelve men, or, more recently, ten men and two women. He and Lyon had been friends for decades, a friendship formed during the Korean War, when Rocco had been a young Ranger officer and Lyon the most junior officer on Division G-2. Their relationship had started with symbiotic necessity; the young intelligence officer needed the eyes and ears of an aggressive patrol leader. Out of this contact a friendship had germinated and still flourished.

They were silent as they sipped their drinks; self-conscious small talk was unnecessary. Rocco slouched farther back on the couch and examined the ceiling.

6

"Ceiling needs painting," he said laconically.

"Probably. Something always needs to be done around here."

"It's turned into a fine house," Rocco said after a slight pause. "A lot of work, but a fine house."

Lyon remembered the day years ago when they had first discovered Nutmeg Hill. It was a fall Saturday, and the brisk air and autumn foliage had dictated an aggressive walk. Lyon and Bea had made their way along the ridge line that ran above the river. Their progress had been slow, impeded by rock formations, heavy shrubbery, and finally by the desolate looming house with boarded windows and doors that perched on the tip of the promontory overlooking the river.

The building had been unused for years. Initially constructed by a sea captain who had made a fortune in the triangle trade, it had suffered through the years by dissolute progeny who committed that prime New England sin—dipping into capital.

"I've got to have it," Bea had said.

"It's been vacant for years," he had replied. "The interior structure is probably completely rotted out."

"Find out, Wentworth. Find out if I can have it," his wife had demanded.

The New York law firm that handled the small remaining trust for the final descendant of the sea captain had been pleased to sell them the house for a price within their range. The interior had been a shambles, but an engineer's report had indicated surprisingly that the basic structure was still sound.

Their work had begun. Room by room, as time and money afforded, they had lovingly restored the house.

"Ceiling still needs painting," Rocco repeated.

"My day has been less than productive," Lyon replied. "You are forcing me into an untenable position."

"I'll get the drop cloths. You have paint in the cellar?"

"We always have paint in the cellar." Lyon went down into the basement for the necessaries, knowing that Rocco's suggestion was partial therapy for both of them. He shrugged as he walked down the steep steps. "So that the day is not a complete loss," he said aloud.

Bea Wentworth circled the supermarket aisles counterclockwise. This sometimes placed her in traffic jams with other grocery carts heading in the more conventional direction, but she insisted on doing her produce shopping last in order to coordinate salad and fresh vegetables with her choice of future main courses. She pondered over fresh mushrooms and delicately began to pluck the most succulent ones from their basket.

She ran a hand lightly over a mound of iceberg lettuce. A faintly perceived pressure seemed to tingle in the small of her back. It was the type of sensation she felt when someone stared at her. She wondered what sort of primeval brain stem still functioned inchoately within her.

Bea whirled.

The aisle behind her was empty except for a young couple who had just wheeled their cart through the front door. They seemed innocent enough. She saw a blurred movement through the plate-glass window, and then it was gone. Had someone been watching her from outside the store? She'd imagined for several days that she was being watched. She shook her head and smiled. Mild paranoia, she thought, probably caused by the upcoming battle over the senate majority leader position. She turned back to the iceberg lettuce.

Bea got in the checkout line with the diminutive blond checker she liked. She bent deep into the cart and began to line up her purchases on the conveyor belt. With her back turned to the front window, she again felt the nearly imperceptible pressure in the small of her back. She shook her head and continued unloading her purchases.

"How are you tonight, Senator Wentworth?" the checker asked with a smile.

"Just fine, Lena. But it's been a long day."

"You know it." The checker quickly finished tabulating

the order, and together they bagged the groceries and loaded them back into Bea's cart.

The shopping center was closing down as the lights in the smaller shops began to wink off. Bea pushed the cart across the nearly deserted parking lot. One of the cart's wheels canted in a crazy angle, and she had to use force to continue her forward momentum.

The story of my life, she thought wryly. Shopping carts with broken wheels and post office lines with people ahead sending outsize packages to Hong Kong. She reached the small red Datsun station wagon, unlocked the tailgate, and swung it upward preparatory to unloading her groceries.

She heard the van door a few spaces away slam and then perceived footsteps rapidly approaching her. She half turned to look over her shoulder.

The approaching man wore jeans, a dark Windbreaker, and a multicolored ski mask pulled down over his face.

Bea instinctively reached into her shoulder bag and fumbled for the container of Mace.

The man's right hand closed over hers, while his left came up toward her face. In the dim light she saw cheesecloth clutched in his fingers. The cloth closed over her face, and she smelled the sweet odor of chloroform.

She turned her head rapidly back and forth to escape the anesthetic cloth and simultaneously brought her knee up into her assailant's groin.

The man gave a mild grunt as her kneecap connected painfully with a hard curved surface at his groin.

A single screaming thought shook Bea. He was wearing a cup!

The cheesecloth was again pressed over her mouth and nostrils—and then blackness.

Rocco and Lyon finished painting the ceiling without appreciable damage to the rest of the room. Rocco carefully folded the drop cloths while Lyon capped the remainder of a gallon of paint.

"I'm hungry," Lyon said. "What time is it?"

Rocco glanced down at the large watch strapped to his wrist with a heavy leather band. "Jesus Christ! It's after ten. Where in the hell is Bea?"

Lyon lifted the kitchen phone off its wall mounting and checked to make sure that the instrument gave off a steady dial tone. It did. The phone was in working order. If she had called they would have heard. "She's probably met someone political and gone for coffee," he said. The words fell hollowly between them. Bea's Thursday-night schedule rarely changed—she was always home by nine or nine-fifteen. She knew he hadn't eaten and would wait until she returned.

"Want that I call headquarters and have the boys on patrol look out for her?"

Lyon shook his head. "I think not. The call would go out over the radio and half the people in Murphysville have scanners—the gossip would be all over town that the senator's husband was looking for his wife."

Rocco nodded. "Makes sense." He began to buckle on his belt with its holstered magnum that he had looped over a kitchen chair. "Why don't we just pop down to the shopping center and see?"

Lyon nodded affirmatively. "The car's probably busted down somewhere between here and there, and I wouldn't want her walking the roads alone this time of night."

Rocco's meaty hand propelled him toward the front door. "Then let's move it!"

They found the small Datsun station wagon parked in the middle of the empty center lot. They sat silently in the car a moment as Rocco splayed the police car's spotlight over the empty car.

"Stop!" Lyon commanded, and Rocco trained the light on the shopping cart nosed against the rear of the vehicle. It was still filled with several bags of groceries. Lyon catapulted from the car and ran over to the cart. Rocco stood behind him with the beam of his powerful flashlight flickering over the bags.

"Over there," Rocco said as he directed the light on a spot just behind the tailgate. "See them?"

Lyon stooped. "Yes." He picked up the key chain. It was familiar; he recognized the car keys, the house key, and several others. He knew it belonged to his wife. "They're Bea's," he announced softly.

Rocco stepped around the side of the vehicle and turned his light into the empty interior. "I wonder how long it's been?"

Lyon felt several items in the grocery bags: a package of steaks, a carton of milk, and a container of ice cream. The milk was lukewarm and the ice cream mushy. "At least an hour," he said.

"Scanners or not," Rocco said, "I think I had better put this on the air."

"I agree," Lyon said. "Let the state police know too."

"Right." Rocco loped over to the patrol car and snatched the transmitter from its stanchion on the dashboard. He began to talk in a low voice.

Lyon listened to his friend's description of Bea and then looked out over the deserted shopping center with its empty parking lot. She was somewhere in the darkness beyond. He tried to will a picture of her, but the only response was a distant streetlight, partially hidden by a high tree, that winked back an indecipherable message.

2

Two cops sat on the edge of the parapet overlooking the Connecticut River. Cops have much in common that transcends their locale. They could have been two cops sitting near the Chicago or Hudson rivers rather than on the patio of a two-hundred-year-old home above the Connecticut River.

"You bring in Flash Warden?" Jamie Martin asked.

"Yeah. Rocco sweated him for two hours, but there's nothing there."

"I always figured Warden for flashing, not abduction."

The other cop responded reflectively through a wad of chewing tobacco. "I don't think the perp comes from around here. I think he's a transient who saw Senator Wentworth and stashed her in his car. Then he took off for the state forest."

"Where he . . ."

"Yeah."

Lyon Wentworth was standing in the doorway within hearing of the two officers on the parapet. His fingers began to tremble, and he felt a weakness in his knees. He turned away from the door and walked over to the bar cart to pour himself another pony of sherry. His chin was stubbled with unshaven beard, and his pants were rumpled from two days' use. He hadn't slept, and the fatigue was beginning to make his mind sluggish. He tossed the sherry down in one gulp, as if it were a shot of cheap bar whiskey, and instantly regretted it. The combination of sleeplessness and anxiety had reduced his tolerance.

A large arm snaked over his shoulder, and he felt Rocco's presence. "You okay, old buddy?"

"How in the hell are you in such better shape than I am?" Rocco had somehow found the time to shave and change his uniform. Lyon knew that the large police officer had had as little sleep as he, but Rocco seemed refreshed and alert.

"I've done this before," Rocco said in a low voice. "After a while you almost get used to it."

"What happened to her, Rocco? It doesn't make any sense."

"The world is filled with crazies, Lyon. They lurk under rocks and pop out when we least expect them."

"I guess." Lyon walked over to the corner of the living room where a large map of the upper portion of the state had been tacked. He bent over to study the streets of Murphysville and then squatted near to get a better look.

They had searched the town until dawn. Rocco's calls had alerted his own men, and the dispatcher had called most of the off-duty patrolmen in to help with the search. Lyon had ridden in the chief's car, hour after hour, using the vehicle's spotlight to search culverts and road shoulders—frightened at what he might find.

"You got the list yet, Wentworth?"

Captain Norbert's voice boomed across the living room and seemed to intrude into every particle of Lyon's being. He felt his body tense as the state police captain moved toward him. "No, not yet," he said, hoping the reply would discourage the man's approach.

"I need the list, Wentworth. I need a list of your wife's enemies."

"My wife is a politician, Captain Norbert. She has a good many friends . . . and enemies."

"This guy want his wife back or not?" The comment was addressed to Rocco at Lyon's side.

"You're out of order, Norbie," Rocco said as he stepped between Lyon and the state police captain.

"Listen, Herbert. I wouldn't even be in on this case so soon if you hadn't begged."

"You're all heart, Norbie. You're really one hell of a sweet fella."

Lyon had seen the two brothers-in-law in argument before. They often seemed on the verge of physical mayhem, but somehow one or the other, perhaps out of deference to Rocco's wife, always retreated from a final confrontation.

"I'll make up some sort of list of names I consider worthwhile following up on," Lyon finally said to dissipate the tension in the room. He turned back to continue his examination of the map. The streets of Murphysville had been combed, searched, and researched. It was the hundreds of acres of state forest abutting the edge of town that concerned Lyon. It was an undeveloped recreational area with miles of unpaved roads, paths, and logging trails. Their search could only be perfunctory with the men available, and yet it was perhaps the most likely area.

He turned abruptly away from the map.

A cacophony of sound seemed to wash over him as if his ears had just become unblocked. In various parts of the living room and dining room, men and women manned phones and radios, their voices vying with each other as they made contact with search units both locally and at the state police barracks. They seemed to eddy in tight groups, as if each feared contamination from the other.

Rocco's men plotted local search routes and made marks on the map as outlying cruisers reported in. The state police monitored the house phone and had direct connections open with all state police barracks and the phone company switching terminal.

Two FBI agents, dressed in dark suits, sat stoically on the couch and seemed to observe everything with a certain silent disdain.

Society had armed itself, but could only wait until contact was made or Bea located; then other experts would replace those assembled here tonight.

The phone rang.

The room fell instantly silent. A state police corporal threw a switch on a recording device and looked up at Lyon expectantly. A woman officer spoke in a low voice to the telephone office.

The phone rang again, and Lyon tentatively picked up the receiver. His palms perspired. "Yes?" His voice was strange to his ears.

"The full resources of the state of Connecticut are behind you, Lyon."

"Thank you, Ruth."

A voice behind him whispered to another officer. "It's the governor."

"I wish she'd get off the goddamn phone," Rocco mumbled.

"I've been in contact with Major Drummond of the state police on this, Lyon," the governor said. "I asked him what else we could do to help Senator Wentworth, and he suggested additional personnel for a search of the state forest in your area. I'm sending in a battalion of the National Guard tomorrow morning to conduct the search."

Lyon's immediate impulse was to thank the governor, but do you thank someone who has just offered to help locate the body of your wife? If she were found in the state forest, she most surely would be dead. "That will help clear matters up, Ruth," he finally said.

"Good! I'll get off the phone now. I just wanted you to know that I'm thinking about you."

"Thank you." He slowly replaced the receiver.

"We're going to get the bastard," Rocco said.

"How?" Lyon retorted, allowing the bitterness he tasted to creep into his voice.

"When he tries to pick up the money," Norbert snapped. "There's no way for him to pick up the ransom without our being there."

"And then someone else kills her," Lyon answered.

"We won't cuff him on the spot, Lyon," Rocco replied. "We put a homing device on the package or we follow him with all sorts of indirect surveillance. Hell, those boys"—he gestured to the FBI contingent on the couch—"are experts on these matters."

Lyon looked thoughtful. "The Amtrak line from New York to Boston runs for over 150 miles through this state. Suppose our mastermind has me ride the train prepared to throw off a valise of money when I receive some sort of light or other visual signal? You can't have men and cars posted along the whole route."

"We'd use a homing device that emits a radio signal. They make them now the size of a medium coin," Rocco said. "We would track the train with planes and helicopters from a suitable safe distance and have guys with you with radios. When the drop was made it would be an easy matter to follow the perp."

"And if he suspects that scenario and changes containers?"

"We also use marked money," Norbert said.

"And asks for tens and twenties equally distributed from several Federal Reserve districts? If he orders that the bills are to be old money and not in sequence?" Lyon suggested.

"They all make mistakes, Lyon," Rocco insisted.

"Somewhere along the line he or she will make a mistake and we'll get them."

The phone sounded shrilly in the crowded room. They froze in position. Rocco arched his eyebrow toward Lyon and nodded toward the phone. Lyon took two hesitant steps and picked up the receiver.

"Wentworth here."

"I've got her."

The voice was inhuman in its pitch and tone. It resembled something manufactured as it spoke in a vibrato that only faintly resembled human speech.

"Who are you?" Lyon clenched the receiver. "Where is my wife, damn it!"

"Safe and sound for the time being, Wentworth. She'll live as long as you follow instructions."

"What instructions? What do you want?"

"You'll find out. I just wanted you to know who has her."

"Who?"

A laugh that sounded more like the whine of machinery. "I know you've called the cops, Wentworth, and it doesn't make any difference. Remember, follow the instructions or she dies . . . painfully."

The phone clicked, and the dial tone hummed in Lyon's ear.

"Is that some sort of machine or what?" an incredulous voice asked from the rear of the room.

"What about the trace?" Rocco snapped.

"I'm getting it," the officer with the earphones said as he talked in a low voice over his headset.

"Play that damn call back," Norbert ordered the officer at the recorder.

"Yes, sir." He rapidly pushed the "rewind" button and in a few seconds the "play" button. The hollow, inhuman voice began again.

"I've got her," it repeated, and the short conversation continued until the sound of the dial tone again filled the room.

"How in the hell did he disguise his voice like that?" Norbert asked.

"A voice box," Lyon said.

"A what?" Norbert asked impatiently.

"A voice box," Lyon repeated. "I'm sure there's a scientific name for them. You've seen them. Cancer patients who have their vocal cords excised learn to speak with them."

Several men in the room who had heard the devices in use nodded assent.

"We'll put a trace on that too," Norbert said. "There can't be but a few medical supply houses who carry an item like that."

"What about the damn trace?" Rocco asked.

"I've got it, sir. A pay telephone on Route 154 near the entrance to I-95."

Norbert and Rocco jostled each other as they bent to examine the map and establish the exact location of the phone. Captain Norbert found it first and placed a finger on the spot, which was near the Connecticut shoreline. "Here it is. That's near the Westbrook Barracks. Get me a phone."

A phone was thrust in the state police captain's hand. He spoke rapidly to the dispatcher at the barracks and handed the phone back to the technician.

"Well?" Rocco asked.

"They're on their way," Norbie announced. "It's a silent run and they'll approach the box from two directions."

"What about the highway?" Lyon asked.

"If he's already on the Interstate, there's nothing we can do to stop him without a vehicle or personal description. We can only hope that he hangs around the area of the phone booth for a few minutes."

"How much time?" Rocco asked.

"We'll know something in five minutes."

It was an interminable wait, and the room was silent except for an occasional cough or movement by one of the waiting officers. The room seemed frozen in a silent tableau, and only Lyon moved as he paced back and forth and finally walked out onto the patio.

The two conversing officers who had sat on the edge of the parapet earlier were now gone, and the patio was empty and dark under a leaden sky.

Lyon sat down heavily on the edge of the stone wall and tried to look down at the river that flowed below. It was a moonless night, and it seemed to enclose the lighted house in a cocoon of silence. Out of the corner of his eye he saw Rocco standing nearby with one foot propped on the wall, a long cigar in his hand.

"We know there's a good chance she's alive," Rocco said. "We know it probably isn't some sex nut who kills wantonly."

"I have the feeling that somehow he knows us, Rocco."

Rocco turned to look at him with professional interest. "You recognized a voice through that damn machine?"

"No, not a particular voice. Perhaps it was a speech pattern, or something else that's subliminal. I just have this feeling that I know him—or did know him."

"But nothing you can definitely place your finger on."

"I wish to God I could."

The phone rang in the living room and both men simultaneously turned and hurried inside. Norbert had the receiver in his hand, muttered an acknowledgment, and slowly hung up.

"They made the phone booth," the state police captain said. "There wasn't a car or pedestrian in the vicinity."

A sigh of disappointment filled the room.

"There was one thing," the captain continued. "Whoever it is left a note."

"A note? Ransom instructions?" one of the FBI agents asked with interest as his first comment of the evening.

"Not quite," Norbert said as he glanced down at his note pad. "It reads, in sum total, 'Ha-ha.'"

Bea Wentworth was more than frightened; dredged from some depth within her, originating in a primitive survival mechanism, was an all-consuming sense of terror.

She had awakened once in the van. She had involuntarily moaned when she found herself strapped to a board-like frame. The van had slowed, evidently pulled off onto the shoulder of the road, and the driver had thrown open the rear doors. The hand with the chloroform-soaked cheesecloth had descended once again.

She had writhed under the tight straps and turned her head violently back and forth. The cloth had pressed down over her mouth and nostrils and been held firmly until she gasped for breath and again drifted into unconsciousness.

It was dark. A deep, unrelieved darkness, and she felt chilled. There was a dank, musty smell to the place where she was confined, but outside of that there was nothing else to indicate where she was held. She strained against the straps that bound her, and although her wrists could lift two or three inches, her ankles were immobile. The surface she lay on was stiff and unyielding.

"Is there anyone there?" Her voice seemed to echo, but there was no response. "Please! Is there anyone there?"

She strained to hear, but a faint drip of water several feet away was the only thing she could hear. The darkness engulfed her without relief.

Where was she and why? She tried to overcome panic and think about what had befallen her. She forced herself to remember the final moments in the shopping-center lot. He had worn a ski mask, and they had fought until she had fallen unconscious. Nothing else; even her remembrance of his physical size was vague.

She had to control herself. She had to fight back the terror and hysteria that began to surface.

20

"Do not think about Wobblies," she said aloud. And, of course, she did.

Two Wobblies, her husband's benign monsters that peopled his children's books, sat in the corner and observed her with fire-red eyes and slowly twitching tails. Their tongues lolled under long snouts, and their stubby bodies swayed in unison.

"It's all a nightmare, and I'm going to wake up in my bed at Nutmeg Hill, right, fellas?"

They shook their heads, and she knew they were telling the truth.

"It's all a horrible mistake, right?"

They wouldn't deceive her and shook their massive snouts again.

She continued talking to the Wobblies, and it helped dispel the terror until she fell into a fitful sleep. She dreamed of doors: doors that opened out of dark rooms that smelled of rotting things; doors that entered onto broad meadows with grass swaying gently in a soft breeze; doors that filled her with exultation when they swung open into a bright noonday sun.

The clank of metal against metal awakened Bea with a start. Terror and panic began to flood through her, but she fought it back with a massive exertion of will. She turned her head toward the sound and saw a sliver of light reach from floor to ceiling.

A flashlight beam bobbed a few feet from her, and then the beam swung rapidly around the room and landed with a blinding flash across her eyes. She squinted into the brightness, trying to make out who held the light.

A door was open behind the light, and she could see the lighter hues of gray in a night sky. Steps near her. The light left her eyes, and again metal clanked against metal. The beam swung across the room to stop at a Coleman lantern on a granite slab. A gloved hand reached for the lantern, pumped the primer a few times, and then lit it.

The gasoline lantern sputtered to life. The gloved hand adjusted the flame until a bright white glow filled the room.

The light hurt her eyes and she strained against the straps that bound her. Then an involuntary moan escaped her as her eyes adjusted and she saw the room that imprisoned her.

She was a prisoner in a crypt.

Three massive stone sarcophagi filled the small vault, and the board on which she was strapped was laid on a fourth.

The man by the lantern turned to face her. It was her attacker from the parking lot. The ski mask hid his face, and he wore the same dark, nondescript clothes. He switched off the flashlight and shifted the small portable cassette recorder he held in his other hand.

"I demand that you unstrap me at once!" Bea said.

"You aren't in any position to demand anything, lady."

"Who are you?"

"Just call me a friend."

"What do you want?"

"You."

"If you're wearing a mask I must know you. Do I know you?"

Her abductor turned and walked to the door. Bea saw that at the entrance there was a barred grille that was ordinarily chained to a heavy hasp by the crypt entrance. A foot before the heavy metal bars was a massive arched metal door leading into the interior. He carefully pulled the door shut and returned carrying a large cardboard box which he placed on one of the stone sarcophagi. He methodically began to unpack items from the container and align them neatly on the stone surface. She watched in detachment as he placed everything in precise rows: several plastic water

22

bottles, canned meats and bread, and a length of chain to which was welded a pair of handcuffs.

He turned to face her, holding the chain in both hands.

"What's that for?"

"To make you more comfortable." He stepped toward the sarcophagus on which she lay. He snapped one handcuff over her right wrist and ran the chain over to the wall, where he padlocked it to a metal ring embedded in the masonry.

He unstrapped her feet and hands and stepped quickly away to the far side of the narrow vault.

Bea swung her feet to the floor and tried to stand. She had to grab for the edge of the sarcophagus in order to keep her balance. She felt light-headed and dizzy.

"Now, isn't that better?" he asked.

"Who are you?"

"Please. Not the same questions over and over again. Are you ready to make a recording for me?"

"On a cold day in hell!" she said as she massaged her legs. The chain clanked as she moved her right hand.

"Then you'll die," he said mildly as he unloaded the last of the food containers.

"I suppose you want money?"

"That's the general idea."

"Where am I?"

"From the looks of it, it would seem that you are chained in a tomb." He began to stuff batteries into the small cassette player.

Bea wondered what she could hit him with. Perhaps she could loop part of the chain over his neck and . . . She would have to wait and bide her time. He was not a large man; she judged him to be about five foot nine and weighing around 150 pounds. He seemed to be in shape. He would be stronger than she.

He finished adjusting the small recorder, inserted a

small microphone cord into its receptacle, and placed the unit down on the sarcophagus. "I would like you to say a few innocuous words to prove that you are alive and well. Then I shall make my presentation to your husband."

"I've got a few words for you, and they all have four letters."

"I'm not in the least interested in your opinion of me, Senator Wentworth; only in your value to your husband." He held the small microphone toward her. "Talk to your beloved," he commanded.

Bea spoke directly into the microphone. "Some creep's got me, Lyon. He's holding me in a crypt, probably somewhere in the state. It's an old place, at least over a hundred years old, and that should narrow it down. The creep wears a mask, but he's about five foot . . ."

Her abductor turned away, took two quick steps to the tape player, and withdrew the cassette. He threw the small reel across the room, where it fell against the wall and clattered to the floor.

"What do you take me for? This isn't a damn telephone you're talking into, it's a tape. Quit with the information and tell him how scared you are."

Bea sat down heavily on the edge of the stone sarcophagus. She had to think. She had to insert something into her short message that would give Lyon a lead. What? And there was so little time.

He turned back to her after reloading the recorder. "Let's get it right this time, little lady. No travelogues. Just tell him how mean I am and how frightened you are. Got that?"

"Yes, I think I do," she said in a low voice.

3

THE MEN IN CAMOUFLAGE suits, combat boots, and fatigue caps were stretched along the tree line in a skirmishers' formation. Sergeants and junior officers behind the long line urged them forward in hoarse voices. The commands echoed from the hills and forced Lyon Wentworth into a rigid posture.

"Spread out! Spread out! Ten feet between each man."

"Watch for newly turned dirt or any article of clothing."

The major standing next to the jeep wore knife-edged fatigues starched in stiff folds. He swung his binoculars rapidly across the moving formation. "I've got some of our Recon people rappeling down the cliffs along the riverbank, Mr. Wentworth. The police are using a boat with grapples to search the water along the edge."

"Sounds thorough," Lyon was finally able to mutter.

"If she's here, we'll find her," the major said with a touch of pride in his voice.

The line of National Guard troops was soon lost from view in a heavy stand of pine. Occasionally a shouted command would reach Lyon, and he came to fear the hearing, for the next shout from the searching men could mean that Bea's body had been located. He kept assuring himself that she was alive, that the phone call from the man with the voice box was valid, and that she was being held some-where.

He turned away from the self-satisfied Guard major and looked down the dirt logging road to their rear. A police cruiser, its dome light flickering, was jouncing in the ruts as it sped toward them at a pace too fast for the road's poor condition. The Murphysville cruiser swerved to a stop a few feet from the jeep.

Rocco Herbert and Captain Norbert erupted from the car.

Lyon watched his friend and the state police officer hurry toward him. Again the fear. Its tentacles sapped the strength of his legs. Behind him he heard the men search-ing in the woods and the voices of command reverberating through the forest. He searched Rocco's face for a sign.

"Any news?" Lyon asked softly.

"That goddamn postmaster is going to be up on charges!" Norbert snapped. "As soon as I can think of the right ones."

"What?" Lyon looked perplexed as he swiveled his gaze from one man to the other.

"We have a man at the post office," Rocco said quickly. "We were waiting for the morning mail, and when yours was sorted, our guy tried to take it."

"Goddamn officious bureaucrat," Norbert mumbled.

"As you can gather, the postmaster wouldn't give us your mail without a court order," Rocco said.

"Where is it now?"

"On its way to your house for delivery. We did get a glance at it. There's a padded envelope addressed to you without a return address."

The three men began to walk rapidly toward the still idling cruiser. "Where was it postmarked?" Lyon asked.

"New York City—Manhattan." Rocco slammed behind the wheel and Norbie climbed in the passenger's side while Lyon sat in the rear seat behind the wire mesh.

"The National Guard will call us at your house if they find anything," Norbert said over his shoulder.

In a series of jerky turns, Rocco turned the cruiser on the narrow logging road until he was headed in the other, direction. He switched on the car's siren when they reached the paved secondary road. The trip back to Nutmeg Hill was a bone-jarring nightmare as Rocco pushed the car to its limits.

When they reached the driveway to his house, Lyon saw the mail jeep parked by his rural mailbox. The diminutive postman was arguing with officer Jamie Martin. "You can't have the mail!" they heard him shout.

The police car rocked to a halt. Lyon fumbled for the nonexistent interior door handles in the rear, while Rocco and Norbert loped toward the mail van. Lyon began to pound on the window to attract Rocco's attention.

Rocco turned sheepishly and returned to release him from the police car.

"I'll take the mail," Lyon said to the indignant mailman.

"I don't know who these guys think they are, Mr. Wentworth," the mailman said as he thrust several letters and the small padded envelope into Lyon's hands.

Lyon glanced through the mail. Several letters that were obvious bills, a letter from his publisher in New York, a few pieces of junk mail, and the package.

"Don't open it," Norbert commanded. "We'll do it properly up at the house."

A state police specialist carefully placed the padded brown envelope on the center of the kitchen table and proceeded to walk a circle around it. He hovered over the package, squatted and stood on his toes, and observed the article from several angles. He finally shook his head in satisfaction and proceeded to remove, with a pair of tweezers, the staples that shut one end. He took care not to touch the body of the envelope. When the last staple was removed, he lifted the envelope with the tweezers and shook it above a small felt pad he had placed on the table.

A mutual grunt went up from the men surrounding the table as a single cassette slid from the envelope and came to a careful rest on the felt pad.

"Bag the envelope and take it for prints," Norbert commanded.

"The cassette too?" the technician asked.

"Wait a minute," Rocco interjected. "I think we had better play the damn thing first."

Norbert nodded. "Get me the recorder from the equipment near the phones."

The technician quickly procured the recorder, plugged it in at the kitchen counter, and lifted the cassette with his tweezers. Carefully, as if defusing a bomb, he placed the tape in the recorder, closed the lid, and pressed the "play" button.

The recorded voice boomed from the small player at a volume that startled everyone. The trooper hastily adjusted the sound. Bea's voice was flat and devoid of feeling. It was as if she were delivering statistical facts on a dry piece of legislation to the state senate.

"He picked me up at the shopping-center parking lot, Lyon, but I suppose you know that by now. I have not been hurt, and he tells me that he will let me eat after this tape is complete." The inflection of Bea's voice changed slightly, and there was a hollow ring to her words. "It would seem prudent for you to do exactly as he says. Please do, Lyon, because I love you and I want to come home to take care of my lilacs."

There was a blank portion on the tape, and then Bea's voice again. "Is that all right?"

"Just fine." The voice that answered had the now familiar whine of machinery in the timber of its inflection. "The lady's location will be revealed when I receive the following stamps express-mailed to: Mr. R. Willingham, Hotel Dalton, 72 Raven Street, London NW 7. The stamps are as follows: four 24-cent inverted airmails, United States; one Hawaiian 2-cent of 1851; one Confederate States of America Mount Lebanon Provisional of 1861; and one Cape of Good Hope 4-pence red color error of 1861. When these stamps are received in England, you will be notified of the lady's whereabouts. You have seven days."

The tape ended.

"Play it again," Lyon said softly.

The technician nodded, rewound the cassette, and again pressed the "play" button. Bea's nearly emotionless voice began.

Lyon Wentworth sat on the kitchen counter and leaned forward with his hands on his knees as he listened intently. "Again," he said when the short tape finished for the second time. The tape was replayed.

"What kind of crap is that? Sending stamps to England?" Norbert snapped.

Raymond Dupress, an FBI agent who had been standing unobstrusively in the corner, looked down at the small pad he held in his hands. "Hardly crap," he said. "I'll make a rough guess that the perp is asking for half a mil."

"What?"

"That's right. Those inverted American airmails must go for nearly a quarter of a million by themselves."

"Are you a collector?" Lyon asked the agent.

"I dabble a bit." The agent laughed. "Nothing on the scale of this guy. That's heavy stuff. Those are some of the most expensive stamps in the world."

"How will he unload them?" Lyon asked.

"There are auctions all over the world," the agent replied. "He can enter them in separate lots under a number. He'll probably spread them out to stamp houses in different countries so that no two appear at the same place. It will be next to impossible to get him, even with Interpol in the act."

"Or he might have arranged for buyers prior to the kidnapping," Lyon said.

"So much for homing devices," Rocco said.

"He still has to pick up the letter and expose himself," Norbert said.

"There's a problem with that tape," Lyon continued.

"What's that?" Rocco asked.

"One, I don't have five hundred thousand dollars with which to buy those stamps; and two, Bea hates lilacs. She has for years."

The command post in the living room had been dismantled, and the police officers had left except for Rocco on the couch and a lone guard by the front door.

"How much sleep have you had since this started?" Rocco asked.

"Not very much."

"I have some yellow jackets at home. Want me to go get them?"

"Some what?"

"Nembutals."

"No, I have to think. Where am I going to get that kind of money?"

"Then you're going to buy the stamps?"

"Of course. If I can figure out a way to do it. We'll worry about catching him later. Right now I want Bea released. I want her safe. I want her home."

"I know you do, Lyon. We all do."

"Five hundred thousand worth of stamps. It may as well be ten million. I looked at our bank accounts a few minutes ago, and you know what? We have eight thousand in the savings accounts, and two in the checking. There's a few shares of stock worth a few thousand more. I'm owed some royalties, and Bea has money in the state retirement fund. I made the list and added it up. We have a net worth of forty-two thousand dollars, and that's one hell of a long way from five hundred thousand or whatever those stamps end up costing me."

Rocco left the couch and walked over to the French door leading to the patio. "How many acres do you have here?"

Lyon waved his hand impatiently. "I don't know."

"Sure you do. You had a survey made."

"I'm not interested in small talk."

"I'll bet you have over fifty acres surrounding Nutmeg Hill."

"Fifty-nine, actually."

"There's your answer."

"What?" Lyon shook his head. "I guess that's a rhetorical 'what'. How much does an acre around here go for?"

"Your property overlooks the river."

"Most of it does."

"Ten thousand an acre, not including the house. The house alone, with access and a few acres, would go for over a quarter of a million dollars."

"In other words, the total parcel of land would be worth over five hundred thousand. I could sell off the acreage and keep the house." Lyon's amazed reaction was ingenuous. He had overlooked the appreciation of their property.

"Yes."

"Do you know of anyone who might be interested?"

"I know a few developers in the area who are always looking for really desirable land—even with the tight money and high-interest situation."

"I'd be appreciative if you would put them in touch— soon," Lyon said.

"Will."

The phone's ring jarred them, and they both stared at the instrument as if it were an unfriendly intruder. Lyon slowly reached for the receiver. "Yes?" He listened a moment and handed it to Rocco.

"Chief Herbert here." Rocco listened for a few minutes, occasionally muttering an "uh-huh." He hung up. "The latest. The Guards finished their sweep through the state forest, and it's negative."

"We knew that from the cassette."

"And a negative on a trace on the voice box and no usable prints on the brown envelope."

"What you're telling me is that we're back to square one."

Rocco walked to the door. "I got to go." He turned abruptly. "What did Bea mean about the lilacs?"

"I don't know. She was trying to tell me something, but I can't figure out what."

"It might come to you if you got some sleep. I'll be back in the morning with any developers I can dig up."

"Thanks, Rocco." The front door slammed and seconds later the police cruiser screeched down the drive at Rocco's usual frenzied pace.

Lyon stood by the bedroom window and wanted a drink, but knew he shouldn't. He wished that he smoked and knew that he couldn't. He was more a man of thought than action, and yet he wanted to drive the roads of Connecticut to look into a thousand faces for his wife. He knew he wouldn't find her. She was invisible. She was stuck away, imprisoned and held in a place he could not see.

"Where are you, Bea?" he said aloud.

She answered him. "Damn it all, Wentworth! Quit kidding around and come get me."

He fell asleep on the couch. It was a restless, troubled sleep. She was somewhere ahead of him and he swung a hedge clipper against the clinging stalks that surrounded him. The smell of ripe flowers was overpowering. He was surrounded by lilacs, and he swung the tool in wide frantic

32

blows to cut his way through the profuse flowers that hid her.

Lyon drank coffee in the breakfast nook and watched Rocco's cruiser careen down the drive. It was followed by a battered and dusty pickup truck of some ancient vintage. Rocco parked, swung from the seat, and leaned in the pickup's window to talk to the driver.

The pickup's occupant stepped out onto the drive and stamped heavily brogaricd feet on the asphalt as if to restore circulation. He was a short, heavy man with a massive head of dirty blond hair. He wore a ripped poplin jacket and work pants stuffed into muddy boots. As he followed Rocco to the front door, he looked from side to side appraisingly.

Rocco smiled when Lyon opened the door. "Lyon, I'd like you to meet Burt Winthrop. Burt's a developer from Middleburg and might have some interest in your property."

"Come on in and have some coffee," Lyon said and led them back to the kitchen. He noticed that Winthrop's trousers were flecked with grease, and he wondered what this man could develop other than an addition to a garage.

"You got a survey map, Wentworth?" the builder asked brusquely.

"Yes. I dug it out this morning." Lyon spread the map over the breakfast-nook table. The two men looked down at it as Lyon served mugs of coffee.

Burt Winthrop handed Lyon his half-emptied mug. He sat down at the table in front of the survey and whipped out a slender pocket calculator from his pocket. His pudgy fingers flew lightly across the keys as he made rapid calculations from his study of the survey.

"If you're interested, I'd have to close tomorrow. I need the money," Lyon announced.

33

Rocco rolled his eyes and pulled Lyon by the sleeve back into the kitchen. He whispered, "Christ, Lyon. Don't make it sound so desperate. This guy will rape you."

"I am desperate, Rocco."

"Close tomorrow?" Winthrop asked when they returned to the nook. "I don't know about that. You got to understand, Wentworth, that I'm just an old country boy, a builder who happened to make a few bucks. I leave the closing thing up to my lawyers."

"That's the way it would have to be," Lyon said.

"Well, I suppose we might do away with a title search and piggyback on the last conveyance. That is if you'll give me full warranties on your deed?"

"Of course."

"Okay, let me give it a few more figures." Again the fingers flew over the calculator. "I could go into my CDs and Treasuries, but I sure hate to touch that money and lose the interest. You got a nice piece of property here, lots of shoreline, but there's plenty of rocks and we'd have to do a lot of blasting. I'd have to squeeze to get enough units in here to make it worth my while."

"Units?"

"Condos."

"Condominiums."

"That's right. I specialize in that. I build mostly for retired folks . . . folks that made a bundle from the sale of their last house and can afford a nice and expensive condo overlooking the water. You understand that a fast close will affect the price. Raising money on short notice is difficult."

"I thought it might affect the price," Lyon said.

"Well, folks," Winthrop said as he stuffed the calculator back in his pocket. "Let's walk around a bit outside."

"I'd like to hold on to the house and a few acres," Lyon said.

"No deal," Winthrop said quickly. "Where you got

34

your house and a couple of surrounding acres plus access would cost me a dozen units."

"I'll give you fifty acres at ten thousand per," Lyon countered. "I keep the house and the remaining land."

The pudgy man shook his head. "No deal. In the first place, your house is on the most desirable site; in the second place, if you keep the house I got to give you an easement to the highway—that cuts the remaining land in half."

"Damn it all, Burt," Rocco said. "This land is worth ten thousand an acre."

"Not if he wants to close tomorrow it isn't." He started to walk to his pickup. "Get another boy. Get someone who'll want an option for sixty days and close in ninety. Four-fifty for everything is tops from me."

"What about the house?" Lyon asked again.

"Including the house. That white elephant is the first thing that goes, Wentworth."

"You'll tear it down?"

"Have to. Four-fifty, close tomorrow. Take it or leave it."

"I'll take it," Lyon said. Lyon looked back at the house. Nutmeg Hill contained so many memories of their marriage, it seemed to radiate a vitality of its own. He knew it had to go; there was no other alternative.

"Four-fifty in certified check, and you'll have it tomorrow at noon in my lawyer's office. This is a real fire sale, isn't it?"

"You might call it that," Lyon answered. He turned away, unable to continue looking at the little man who was going to tear down their house in order to build as many condominium units as he could legally squeeze onto the property. He felt rage. They, whoever they were, were taking everything without reason. His wife, their home, all they possessed. He wanted to fight, to take physical action of any sort that would relieve some of the pain and frustration.

He had left and taken the lantern with him. The darkness, with its attendant fears, was worse than his menacing presence. Bea stretched the chain that held her fast to the wall to its fullest extent, and felt her way along the dank walls. She could feel along three walls of the crypt, but the fourth, which contained the entrance, was out of reach.

She moved her hand lightly across the sarcophagus that held the food and water supplies. Her hand closed over a water container, and she raised it to her lips and drank greedily until water spilled out the side of her mouth and ran in a thin rivulet across her chin and down her neck.

She worked her way back through the darkness to her pallet and sat down. The chain clanked on the floor by her side. Her limbs felt leaden, her shoulders slumped forward, and she wanted to cry.

She realized with a start that she wanted her captor to return. She actually yearned for contact, stimuli, any conversation, no matter how dire. Anything that would give relief from the darkness that surrounded her.

She wasn't sure if it was an hour or a day later when she heard sounds at the door.

He slipped the padlock in his back pocket and forced back the heavy hasp on the grillework. As always, the heavy grille before the crypt door was hard to move on its ancient hinges. He applied both hands and pushed it back against the stonework and slowly opened the arched interior door.

As the door cracked open, it cast a swatch of light across the stone floor. He heard the chain rustle. There was a sigh from his prisoner. He gave a tight smile and turned for a final look at the graveyard.

The plot was empty as always. Only once during his many visits to the place had he discovered a visitor, an old lady busily making grave rubbings from some of the older stones. She had soon left and had not returned.

The church that had once served this place of the dead had burned down thirty years ago, and the rural inhabitants, sparse in number with the demise of farming in Connecticut, had not seen fit to rebuild their house of worship. The cemetery was now unused and forlorn, a very suitable place for his purposes.

He slipped inside the crypt. The Coleman lantern was immediately inside the door and available to him as he stepped inside, but out of her reach. He gave the lantern a few pumps and lit the wick.

If he was going to rape her, this would be his last opportunity. He would savor the moment.

She was sitting on the floor with her knees drawn to her chin. The bright glow was too strong, and she shielded her eyes.

Thoughts of sexual attack fled. She looked god-awful. Her face was already gaunt. Her eyes were sunken surrounded by dark rims of fatigue. She reminded him of a raccoon he had once seen caged in front of a gas station along a highway in South Carolina.

"Please let me go," she said.

"Your husband has the instructions. If he comes across as told, you'll be out of here in a week."

"A week!" She pulled her knees closer to her chin and seemed to shrink in size. "I can't live in here a week."

"That's up to you, lady." He turned and went back outside for the containers of water he had piled along the wall. He placed them alongside the remaining food.

"I'll see that you get money and I won't help the police come after you."

"Yah, you got to be kidding."

"I am very serious."

"Well, so am I. Your husband gets the letters with your location when I get my stamps."

"We don't have that kind of money."

"He's got lots of friends. You're not the spunky lady I saw prancing around the statehouse, are you?"

"No."

"I'm glad you're humble. It's good for the character."

"You're a sadistic son of a bitch," she said in a low voice.

"Now, Senator Wentworth, don't get me angry or I'll cut your water supply in half."

"You're sweet."

"Now listen to me, little lady. And you had better listen good. I have researched this thing very thoroughly. The human body can sustain itself for up to three months without food, and less than three days without water. You have a week's water here if you ration yourself to a pint a day. You have food for nearly that time. If you don't make a pig of yourself. Do you understand?"

"Will you leave me the lantern?"

He hadn't planned to. He mentally calculated what possible ways she could use it, except for its intended purpose. "Why not? There's only a few hours of fuel left, so you had best conserve it." He tossed down a package of book matches next to the lantern. "Remember, you have a week." He knew it should be only five days, but he wasn't going to tell her that and make it easy for her. "Take it easy now," he said and left.

He closed the double doors to the tomb and relocked the padlock. He stripped off the rubber gloves he had been wearing and stuffed them into his back pocket. He walked down the hill to the van parked on the country road by the gates to the cemetery.

He slid into the seat of the van and flipped open the glove compartment. The letter, written a week before the kidnapping, was addressed and stamped. He lifted it gingerly from its resting place by grasping the edges. It was addressed to Lyon Wentworth, RFD, Murphysville, Connecticut, and did not contain a return address. The typed instructions inside located the cemetery and vault. He had dropped the portable typewriter into the depths of Bantam Lake. The letter would be mailed tomorrow in Atlanta, just before he caught indirect flights to London.

He estimated that the letter would arrive in Connecticut two or three days after mailing. By the time Wentworth got it, either he would have already mailed the stamps to London or he wasn't going to. No matter, it was a risk he had taken into consideration. He felt that the odds were heavily favorable that Wentworth would come up with the necessary money one way or the other.

That bastard would get his wife back either way, but he wouldn't know that until the last possible moment.

He flipped the envelope onto the passenger's seat next to the ski mask. He threw the van in gear.

The ski mask!

He turned off the ignition and pounded the steering wheel in frustration. How could it have happened? He had planned everything so carefully. All had gone exactly as planned, and now for this to have happened. . . .

He had gone into the crypt the last time without wearing the mask.

She had seen him full face by the light of the Coleman lantern!

He turned and looked through the rusted fence up the hill toward the crypt at the apex of a small rise. She was now securely chained and locked inside, and yet, once released, she would be able to identify him.

Everything for nothing! It had all come apart.

He left the van and stood by the gates as the wind ruffled his chair. Of course he would have to kill her.

The only weapon he had with him was a small pocket penknife. It would be a messy and bloody affair, one that would give him nightmares during the plush days ahead.

That would not be necessary.

He turned and looked back inside the van. The letter telling of her location, the one he intended to mail in Atlanta, still nestled on the seat. He reached inside and crumpled it as he brought it toward him.

He ripped the letter into two dozen pieces, threw them in the air, and watched the breeze blow them out over the meadow.

She would die, of course, but then, that was the way it had to be.

He got back inside the van and restarted the engine. There was plenty of time to catch the flight to Atlanta. After all, he had planned it all so carefully.

4

Lyon typed the envelope with two careful fingers:

Mr. R. Willingham
Hotel Dalton
72 Raven Street
London NW 7
England

He carefully removed the envelope from the typewriter, folded a piece of blank paper which would hide the
stamps from outside view, and slipped the paper into the
envelope. He put the envelope into the inside pocket of his
sport coat.

It was time to go. He switched off the typewriter and
left the room.

He paused in the hallway as if listening to her voice.
The house was quiet, and yet filled with Bea's presence as if
she still occupied the rooms. He hurried down the hall and
out the door toward the car waiting in the drive.

Two cars bracketed his on Route 15 as he approached
the entrance ramp to the Interstate. He honked and waved
them away, but the other car's occupant motioned for him
to pull over on the shoulder. He jammed his foot on the
accelerator and the small Datsun jumped ahead.

Their speed matched his as they continued their frantic waving. He slowed, and the police cruiser to his right signaled to him. He swerved to pull off on the dirt shoulder. Lyon angrily slammed from the station wagon.

"What is this? I'm in a hurry to get to New York City."

"Chief wants to see you," Patrolman Jamie Martin said.

"I don't have time."

"He said to meet him at Sarge's Place," the uniformed officer insisted.

"And if I don't, you guys are going to stop me."

"Something like that." Martin grinned.

"I don't think it's funny," Lyon said as he returned to the Datsun. He backed off the shoulder and reversed direction. It was nearly noon. Of course Rocco would be at Sarge's; he always was at this time of day.

Lyon had long ago decided that Sarge's Bar and Grill was a whimsical masquerade of a real drinking establishment. Sarge Renfroe, a retired army master sergeant who had once served as Rocco's 'First,' had decided that knowing a town's police chief was an excellent reference for operating a gin mill, although he rarely served gin to his shot-and-a-beer customers. Sarge ran the establishment as a cross between a servicemen's beer club at a remote army post and an off-limits Korean "hooch." The scarred tables and booths were of prehistoric vintage, and the bar stools seemed to have been planted a century ago. Dusty bottles of never-eaten pickled pigs' feet and hard-boiled eggs decorated the shelf behind the bar.

Rocco usually lunched at Sarge's because for a dollar the ex-noncom provided him with a large stein of beer and a hamburger on a soft roll. The thick, juicy burger was undoubtedly the best in the state. Six months ago Lyon had discovered Sarge's secret. He had accidentally gone in the small back room and caught Sarge grinding up prime steak for Rocco's exclusive hamburger. He estimated that Sarge lost three dollars on every hamburger he served the large police chief. Lyon had never informed on Renfroe and could only stare jealously at Rocco's succulent hamburger as he devoured his own of more mundane quality.

Lyon marched through the front door, picked up the glass of sherry from the bar that Sarge automatically poured for him, and plunked himself into the booth opposite Rocco. "It had better be important," he said. "I'm on my way to New York to pick up the stamps."

Rocco consumed the last of his hamburger in a large final bite and washed it down with a gulp of beer. Lyon noticed that the chief was in a suit rather than his usual uniform.

"Got something for you," Rocco said. "I didn't want you to go without it." He reached into his pocket and handed a folded check across the table.

Lyon let the check lie before him. He looked down at it with dread. "What's this?"

"Refinanced the house," Rocco said as he drank the remainder of his beer and signaled to Sarge for a refill. "It's remarkable the way real estate has appreciated. I got an additional forty, but I had to take twenty-five hundred for expenses."

"Closing costs?"

"No. For my trip to London."

Lyon opened the check to see that it was in the amount Rocco had indicated. "You can't do this."

Rocco shrugged. "What the hell. We'll catch the bastard and get all our money back."

"And if we don't?"

"Then I continue paying on the damn house until I'm eighty-five." He leaned across the table. "You know, I don't think the bank's very smart. I don't think I'm going to live to be eighty-five."

Lyon reached into his own pocket and withdrew the London envelope and a check of his own. He handed the check across the table. "I never thought there was that

43

much money in the world, much less that Bea and I were worth that much."

"You closed on Nutmeg Hill?"

"Yesterday afternoon. I have thirty days to vacate. I'll worry about that when Bea is back. Rocco, you can't use your own money to go to England."

"The town of Murphysville isn't going to foot it. I took a week off and have already talked to an inspector at Scotland Yard. He promised to help in every way he could."

"I can't let you."

Rocco squinted. "I'm going to be there when he picks up those stamps, Lyon. I'm going to be right there."

Lyon stood. "I have to go. It's over a two-hour drive to the city." He handed Rocco's check back. "I have enough, but thanks."

Rocco gestured. "Sit down. We're going down together, with the dome light on. We'll make it in less than two hours. I've made arrangements with the NYPD to take the letter by special car to the airport, along with yours truly. The letter and I will be on the same flight to London."

Lyon sat down and gestured to Sarge. The thirty-year-man shuffled around the bar and over to the booth. "Rocco wants another hamburger, and I'll have a Dry Sack."

Renfroe nodded and ambled over to the grill.

"I can't eat another bite," Rocco said with a puzzled look.

"This one is for me," Lyon said.

"Have you had any thoughts?"

"Dozens," Lyon replied. "But nothing that's any good. That remark about the lilacs keeps going around my head. Bea was telling me something, but I don't know what. If I could only get a handle on what she meant."

"Norbie's useful for once," Rocco said. "The state police have requested all the flight manifests for planes flying to England for the whole week. I'll see that you get copies.

44

One of the names just might be familiar, and you did say that you might have known the man."

Lyon shook his head. "He could be traveling under a false passport, or what about connecting flights, say a flight to Amsterdam with a connector to London?"

"I have a feeling we can narrow it down even further, but I will call Norbie about the connector flights."

"How's that?" Lyon asked.

"I figure the perp is a stamp collector. He's got to be pretty damn sophisticated in that area to know how to lay off the stamps once he has them. He had to know which ones to demand."

"Of course," Lyon said. "He's got to be a collector, which means he probably belongs to the American Philatelic Society and subscribes to the *American Philatelist Journal*."

Rocco nodded with a smile. "You've been doing your homework. Now, let's say that we get a copy of the APS *Journal* subscription list, which I understand is about fifty thousand, and cross-check that against the plane manifests?"

"We might come up with a list of duplicate names."

"Odds are that only a few names will appear on both lists."

"It's worth a try," Lyon said.

"It'll give you something to do until I get back or we hear from the perp."

Her voice suddenly seemed to fill the room, and Lyon lurched back against the rear of the booth as if struck.

"It is my feeling that a state income tax is the only equitable way to levy our tax obligations on a fair basis," Bea Wentworth said. "As it stands now, we are in effect overburdening the poor to the benefit of the rich."

"Bea . . ." Lyon said.

"Those were the last recorded words of the popular

Senator Beatrice Wentworth," a male voice said. "She has now been missing for—"

"Turn that damn television off!" Rocco bellowed.

"Let's get out of here," Lyon said.

They reached New York in under two hours and double-parked in front of a brownstone on Fifty-ninth Street. Lyon looked at the address and then up at the building. It took him a few moments to locate the discreet brass plaque next to the doorbell that simply announced, "Brumby, Philatelists." He gestured to Rocco, and they climbed from the car.

Lyon heard muted chimes toll within the brownstone after he rang the bell. The door was immediately opened by a white-maned man dressed in an impeccable pinstripe suit with a carnation in his lapel. He gave a sonorous "Yes?"

"I have an appointment with Mr. Brumby," Lyon said. "The name is Wentworth."

"Mr. Brumby is expecting you, Mr. Wentworth." He cast an oblique glance at Rocco.

"This is my associate, Mr. Herbert," Lyon said as they followed the man inside.

The main hallway had been widened and carpeted with Turkish rugs, and display cases were arranged every few feet. Paintings from the Hudson River School adorned the walls and were illuminated by recessed overhead lights. On top of each display case filled with stamps was a magnifying glass, aligned neatly next to a piece of felt. Two patrons sat on high upholstered stools before the display.

Lyon and Rocco were ushered into a paneled office with bookshelves filled with stamp catalogs and were seated in side chairs before a vacant oak desk. Out the rear window Lyon could see a well-tended rose garden.

A door closed quietly behind them.

"Mr. Wentworth. I am Edward Brumby."

They shook hands, and Lyon introduced Rocco as his associate. Edward Brumby wore a three-piece suit of the same cut, but obviously more expensive, as that of the floor manager who had met them at the door. He was a rotund man with tufts of soft white hair growing spasmodically on either side of his head. Round, heavy glasses made his face appear even more symmetrical than it was. He was a short man of considerable girth and slow, precise movements.

Brumby sat behind the desk and spoke softly as he removed a piece of felt and a list of stamps from the center desk drawer. "You must be an insatiable collector, Mr. Wentworth, to request such beauties as these?"

"Not really," Lyon answered and wondered how long this session would continue.

"You were perhaps recommended by one of the Boston Wentworths?"

"No." Another highly placed source, Lyon said and thought to himself, Ray Dupress of the FBI Dupresses.

"Yes. We at Brumby consider ourselves the Tiffany of philatelists." He searched through a vest pocket and extracted a stamp encased in a small acetate envelope. He placed it reverently on the center of the felt and handed Lyon a magnifying glass. "Ah, such a stamp. The Hawaiian 2-cent of 1851. A rare beauty. A gem for any collector."

Lyon glanced quickly at the stamp. "I can assume the authenticity of this stamp?"

"Mr. Wentworth! Our whole reputation stands behind our sales."

"I'm sure it does."

Brumy glanced back at the list of stamps. "Ah, yes. Four 24-cent inverted airmails." He searched his pocket and again brought forth a clear envelope containing the stamps. "The inverted airmails. Such drama. You know, of course, the story? Mr. W. T. Robey on May fourteenth, 1918, brought a block of one hundred at the post office. He immediately recognized their worth, and today they are priceless."

Lyon was getting edgy. "Were you able to obtain all of the stamps on the list I phoned?"

"But of course." Brumby glanced down at the list. "I had to pay premium prices. Your time schedule did not allow me to try foreign sources or the usual auctions." He began to check the list with a small gold pen. "One Confederate States of America Mount Lebanon Provisional of 1861, one Cape of Good Hope 4-pence red color error of 1861. Yes, the list is complete." He continued rummaging in his pockets and produced the other stamps. He spread them all out on the felt. "For your examination."

"Fine." Lyon scooped up the stamps and stuffed them into the London envelope.

"Mr. Wentworth. Really! Your attitude toward those precious items is most cavalier. What sort of collector are you?"

"Well, actually I'm not a collector."

"These stamps are being used as kidnap ransom," Rocco interjected.

Edward Brumby stared at them incredulously. "Ransom? Then you are the Wentworth from Connecticut who's been on television."

"My wife," Lyon answered.

Brumby continued staring at them in amazement. "Of course, I must ask that you return those stamps. The firm of Brumby and Company will not be a party to any such nefarious undertakings. I will not allow those items you hold to be desecrated by criminal elements."

Rocco turned away. "Oh, Jesus God," he said in a low voice.

"I have a certified check for the price," Lyon said.

"I am perfectly willing to forgo my commission on this matter and resell the stamps at auction," Brumby replied.

"Mr. Brumby, unless these stamps are sent to an overseas address immediately, my wife's life will be in deep jeopardy."

"We may have to fight our way out of here," Rocco mumbled.

"Besides," Lyon continued, "I am positive that the culprit intends to resell these stamps at once. So, as you can see, they will shortly be back in the hands of true collectors who will appreciate their value."

"Well, that is a good point," the stamp dealer said. "I can understand your concern, Mr. Wentworth, but it is so distasteful."

"It is for all of us," Rocco said.

"You can be of further help, sir," Lyon said. "When he receives these stamps, how will he get rid of them for profit?"

"Well, he could have already made arrangements with a private collector, or he could work through one of the large houses."

"There can't be many of them," Lyon said.

Brumby beamed. "Oh, with currencies being what they are, and a rather unstable market in diamonds and gold, stamps are a fine investment. More and more money is poured into them, even by the Arabs."

"Just our luck," Rocco said.

"Where and how?" Lyon pressed.

"It would have to be a large auction house to carry such a consignment, and the lot should probably be broken up and sold separately. Now, if I were doing it"—he was apparently beginning to relish the details of the scheme—"I would sell the four 24-cent inverteds through H. R. Harmer in New York, the Cape of Good Hope through Robson Lowe in London, and the Confederate Provisional through Edgar Mohraman in Hamburg. Of course, there are many other fine houses who could carry the consignment!"

"Can it be done through a blind submission?"

"Surely. They could be handled through a Swiss bank account. You know, of course, that counterparts to these very same stamps are due for auction within the next two weeks?"

"No," said Lyon, "we didn't know."

"I would say," Brumby continued, "that it will be nearly impossible to check back on them. Whoever it is will clear a fortune." There was a buzz, and Brumby picked up a phone bracketed out of sight behind his desk. He spoke in a low tone for a few moments and then hung up with a scowl. "It would seem that there are several policemen on the display floor."

"They are waiting for me," Rocco said. "I told them I would meet them here."

"Most unsavory," Brumby said as he accepted Lyon's check. "Most."

Within five minutes Rocco had taken the sealed envelope containing the stamps from Lyon and was riding with his police escort to Kennedy International Airport. Lyon was behind the wheel of the Murphysville police cruiser and swerving through the madness of Manhattan traffic.

Lyon drove without conscious thought up Manhattan and across the South Bronx. Only in the Bronx was he aware of his surroundings when he glanced out the car window and saw the shells of buildings and the burned testament of a society turned inward in a rampage of self-hate.

As he approached the Connecticut Turnpike, he cringed back against the seat as if physically feeling the pain Bea might be suffering. The solution had to do with lilacs. She had told him as much, and he still couldn't fathom what she meant.

5

LYON WENTWORTH DREAMED OF lists. In his sleep he ran his fingers down endless columns of computer printouts. The list seemed to stretch forever as it fell over his feet, ran through the door of the study, and down the hall and through the French door onto the patio. And still it continued. He moaned and ran his fingers down the long lists, mouthing each name to see if it struck a chord of familiarity.

The FBI had compiled the lists and provided the state police and Lyon with duplicate copies. The agent named Dupress had been succinct: "We'll run the names for possible MOs and Wanteds. We want you to see if you know anyone."

The lists were compiled from two sources: plane manifests of flights to London or other cities in Europe that might provide connector flights to London; and the subscription list of the *American Philatelic Journal*. He was to pick up names on the manifests and compare them to the other list.

Lengthy groups of Williamses, Smiths, Browns, and Whites complicated the task.

He dragged himself from sleep and blinked open his eyes. The list dream was still vivid. He moaned. Not only had all day yesterday been spent on the lists, and all of today was so destined, he had done it in his sleep. He rolled out of bed and staggered toward the shower.

He sat in the breakfast nook with a mug of coffee in front of him, the lists to one side, and a yellow legal pad for notes on the other. Sun shone through the window and dappled the walls of the brightly lit room. It was a lovely day completely alien to his mood.

He sipped coffee and said aloud, "The bastard probably used a forged passport." He stared at the ceiling and reviewed the process of obtaining a passport. A birth certificate. You need only check the newspaper obits for the death of someone your own age and write to the Bureau of Vital Statistics with the proper fee in order to get a new copy. Passport photographs and an application under the assumed name, and in days you had a passport under a new identity.

Too easy, but in this instance would it even be necessary? That was the slim hope they had to work on. He bent over the lists again.

At ten o'clock he found an unmistakable name that was familiar. "R. Traxis," he said aloud. Possibly it belonged to Robert Traxis of Connecticut. He picked up the subscription list for the stamp journal and hastily searched it for Traxis.

It was there. His fingers trembled as he underlined it. Robert Traxis, 7 Overview Drive, Wessex, Connecticut. The coincidences were remarkable: Not only had R. Traxis flown to London on the Concorde several days ago, he was also a stamp collector. Most important of all, he was Bea's most virulent and dedicated political opponent.

Lyon spilled coffee as he rushed to the kitchen phone. He flipped the phone from its cradle and began to punch numbers.

He stopped. Rocco was gone, and there wasn't any evidence to present to the heavy-handed Captain Norbert. He would make the investigation himself. Where did Traxis work? He owned a medium-sized industrial concern of some sort down near the Connecticut shore. What was its name?

He dialed information and then the number.

"Traxis Machine Company," an alert female voice answered.

"Can you please tell me where Mr. Traxis can be reached in London? I have an urgent message for him."

"Mr. Traxis returned from Europe last night. We expect him in the office later today. If you will leave your name?"

Lyon felt numb. It was too early for him to have returned from England. It was too soon for the stamp delivery. Rocco would have called if any contact had been made.

"Hello. Are you there?" the voice from the machine company pressed.

Lyon glanced at the Concorde's flight manifest. Traxis, if he was presently at home, had been in Europe less than twenty-four hours. "Does Mr. Traxis fly to England often?"

"Oh yes, sir. Constantly. We have a plant near Birmingham."

"I see. Thank you. Oh, could I please have his home phone number?"

"I am sorry, but that number is unlisted. If you will leave a message?"

"Thank you. I'll call back." Lyon slowly hung up. He tapped the wall impatiently. Continuing to go over the endless lists of names was impossible; it was time to do something. He lifted the phone again and dialed the Murphysville Police Headquarters and asked for Jamie Martin.

"Good morning, Mr. Wentworth," Jamie answered with a sense of relief in his voice. "For a minute I was afraid it was another housewife who wanted to be locked up."

"I need an unlisted phone number. The name is Robert Traxis; he lives in Wessex."

"Is it a police matter?"

"Something Rocco wanted me to follow up on."

Lyon could sense the officer's hesitation, but then he said, "I'll get it from the phone company and call you back."

Bea Wentworth watched the sputtering Coleman lantern in horrified anticipation. It was running out of fuel, and there wasn't any more in the small stock of provisions remaining. In minutes she would be in total blackness.

She couldn't turn away from the failing lantern. She could put up with almost anything, including her imprisonment, but not the total dark.

How long had he been gone? She glanced down at the small diamond-chip watch Lyon had given her last Christmas. It read 2:23. Day or night? Good God, she couldn't be sure, and now she was uncertain as to how long she had been held here.

She had once read of an American prisoner of war who had spent a good deal of time in solitary confinement. In order not to go mad, he had spent the time mentally building a dream house.

That was what she would do. She would rebuild Nutmeg Hill from the beginning.

Bea closed her eyes and recalled the first day she and Lyon had stumbled across the boarded house. She relived the day of the closing and that afternoon when they had entered the house knowing it was theirs.

The house had been a shambles. Over the years the boarded windows had developed chinks, and an assortment of debris had forced itself through tiny apertures. The hardwood floors were deeply rutted, as if teams of cleated sportsmen had performed complicated folk dances on them. Bea would have cried at the condition if she hadn't been so happy to have possession of their white elephant.

Just as they had started with the long center room, now their living room, so did Bea begin in the darkness the slow, methodical task of mentally refurbishing Nutmeg Hill.

Wessex was only a twenty-minute drive from Murphysville, and Lyon would have been stopped for speeding if any state troopers had clocked him. He slowed as he approached the village and down-shifted as the car turned into Main Street and the center of town.

One of the oldest towns in the state, Wessex had once been a small but thriving seaport located a few miles above the mouth of the Connecticut River. The town had slept from the demise of whaling until after World War II, when it had been "discovered." Due to the combination of the passing time and a vigorous historical society, the original nineteenth-century facade of the village center had been preserved.

Wessex differed from most New England towns in that it was not centered around a green, but radiated from the small harbor that had once been its hub.

He parked in front of the Captain's House that was the Traxis address. The house itself was a freshly painted white with a widow's walk on its slate roof. Its long leaded glass windows were shrouded from the inside by lined draperies. Around the corner of the house Lyon saw a well-kept lawn that led down to the water at the edge of the harbor.

He left the car, walked the few steps to the door, and pressed the doorbell. A chime rang in the interior of the house.

He thought back to the last time he had seen Robert Traxis.

In order to gain popular support for the controversial passage of a bill increasing welfare benefits, Bea Wentworth had her committee hold public hearings in various parts of the state. One of those meetings had been held at the Wessex Junior-Senior High School.

Robert Traxis had gained early possession of the floor

microphone and had dominated the hearing with a long speech on individualism, Americanism, welfare fraud, and a host of related topics that culminated in a patriotic plea whose code words were a suggestion that if "they" didn't like it, let them leave.

Bea had impatiently snorted from the podium and spoken an aside to a fellow senator that was amplified throughout the auditorium: "What he really means is that everyone should go out and inherit a factory."

The remark had released the audience's pent-up tension over the Traxis diatribe, and they had burst into laughter.

Robert Traxis had never forgiven Bea, and since that day he had devoted time, energy, and money to her defeat or embarrassment. He was a logical candidate for Bea's worst enemy.

The door was opened by a blond man with hair nearly white who appeared to be in his mid-twenties. He wore a T-shirt that exposed well-muscled arms and shoulders, sweat pants, and New Balance running shoes. "Yeah," he said in a flat voice. His slate-gray eyes were hard.

"I want to see Traxis."

"He's in the gymnasium and is never disturbed."

"It's important. I'm coming in one way or the other," Lyon said in a quiet voice.

"Really." The slate eyes appraised him. "Okay, what's your name?"

"Wentworth."

"Come in." The eyes flicked to the side of the door as he drew it back. Lyon stepped into the narrow hallway with its highly polished hardwood floors. "He gets mad as hell if I break into his workouts."

"Ask him."

The man shrugged and padded silently down the hall into the far recesses of the house. The facade of the building that fronted on the street was deceptive. The house extended far to the rear, with a dozen first-floor rooms opening off the hall. Midway down the hall, a steep stairwell rose to the second floor, while on the walls framed paintings of sea captains stared unemotionally out of past centuries.

Lyon wondered how many of the grim-faced men on the wall had engaged in the lucrative slave trade. He knew that many venerable Northeast fortunes had been started that way and then converted to respectability through the emergence of nineteenth-century textile plants. These fortunes were now snugly harbored in stocks and bonds and managed by very conservative trust officers.

The pale man appeared at the far end of the hall and gestured to Lyon to follow him.

Robert Trainor Traxis was dressed in a gray sweat suit and was on his back doing leg exercises within the maze of a Universal gym. Lyon stood ten feet behind him as Traxis finished his set and let his feet fall to the floor. A large sweat V stained the front of his sweat shirt.

"What in the hell do you want, Wentworth?"

"I want to talk to you about my wife."

Traxis flipped over and did rapid push-ups and then scrambled lightly to his feet in a lithe movement that belied his fifty years. He was a chunky man with a completely bald head and a physical vitality that seemed to permeate his body. His facial features were flat and expressionless, and his eyes were cold. "I don't play the hypocrite, Wentworth. I know your wife is missing, and that's too bad, but don't ask me to bleed for her."

Lyon felt a well of anger rise into his dry mouth. He fought to retain his composure. "I would hardly come here for any sympathy, Traxis."

"Then why are you here? I run a tight schedule, and I have to shower, change, and be back at the plant within the hour."

Lyon mentally reviewed what information concerning

Bea's disappearance had been released to the media. He knew the fact that the ransom payment was in stamps had been withheld, as had the London drop-off. "I understand you make frequent trips to England?"

"Very frequent." Traxis snapped a towel around his shoulders and walked briskly from the room, with Lyon following. The man who answered the front door stayed behind to straighten up the small gym. "I have a factory in England. If you want a travel guide, the local library is well equipped to answer your questions."

They walked down the hall to a sunroom where a silver pot of coffee waited on a glass-topped table.

"I'm interested in how many stamps you might have purchased in London," Lyon said.

"Coffee?" Lyon shook his head. Traxis poured some into a bone china cup and added cream. "A good part of my collection has come from London. What in the hell is this, Wentworth? What devious little scheme is in the back of your teeny liberal mind?"

"Do you own an inverted American airmail?"

"I do not. And I'd give my right arm for one. I specialize in early airmails, you know. This conversation seems built on non sequiturs. What in the world would an inverted airmail have to do with your wife's . . ." He stopped with his cup poised in midair. "She's being held for ransom and they're asking for stamps."

"Four 24-cent inverted airmails, a Hawaiian 2-cent of 1851, a Confederate Mount Lebanon—you are familiar with those stamps?"

"Hell, any serious collector in the world is. They are some of the most valuable in existence."

"And they are to be delivered in London," Lyon continued.

There was a pause from the man at the glass-topped table. "I don't like it one goddamn bit, Wentworth. I know what you're thinking."

"Your name is the only one I recognize that appears on the subscription list of the *American Philatelic Journal* and certain plane manifests."

A small muscle throbbed in Traxis' left cheek as he stared at Lyon. "I can guess the scenario," he finally said. "I, due to my all-consuming hatred of Bea Wentworth combined with a desire to accumulate certain valuable stamps . . . You are full of it. You are as full of it as your wife."

Lyon felt a flush of anger so strong that his legs and knees felt weak, and he had a desire to hold on to something for support. He fought for control. "When are you going back to England?"

"None of your damn business."

"Tomorrow? The day after?"

"As a matter of fact, I wouldn't be in Wessex today if it wasn't required for the annual board meeting. I am returning to England in the very near future." He placed his coffee cup firmly in its saucer and stood. "When was your wife taken?"

Lyon told him.

"If it will get you off my back, it so happens that on that particular evening I was at a town meeting. As usual, I made my views known. I estimate that I was seen and heard by over a hundred people."

"That's easily verifiable."

"Yes, isn't it?" He called out, "Reuven!" Almost immediately the younger man appeared in the doorway. "Please show my friend here to the door. Our business is concluded."

Reuven looked at Lyon, who rose and followed him down the hallway.

Lyon stopped with his hand on the front door. "By the way, Reuven, where were you last Thursday?"

"Right here. I polished silver that night."

"All alone?"

"All alone."

*   *   *

Lyon sat in the car and wished Rocco were with him. He was certain that the large police chief, because of his experience, would have conducted a more productive interview. This one had accomplished nothing. Traxis collected stamps and periodically went to England. Both enterprises were perfectly legitimate. He had probably collected stamps since he was a boy, and he apparently had an airtight alibi for the night Bea was taken.

On the other hand, Traxis did dislike Bea with a nearly unreasonable passion, seeing her as representative of a whole political spectrum that he not only hated, but considered a threat to his interests. Moreover, Traxis had money, and nearly any service could be obtained for a price.

Lyon drove the two short blocks to the town hall, where he quickly scanned the minutes of the last town meeting. Traxis had indeed been present, and his remarks at the meeting were noted.

That left the man with the gray eyes.

6

LYON'S HANDS PERSPIRED as he snicked the phone from its
wall bracket. "Wentworth," he said flatly.

"He got away."

"Rocco?"

"Yes."

"Where are you?"

"At an infirmary somewhere in London."

"Are you all right?"

"A few cuts from flying glass, nothing major. Might
even improve my looks."

"What happened?"

"As you know, the letter was addressed to Willingham
at the Hotel Dalton on Raven Street. I had all sorts of coop-
eration from the Yard and they had men staked out in the
street, and one of their guys posed as the room clerk. We
had a crew, including me, in a room across the street.
Willingham, whoever he is, had reserved a room in the
hotel by mail. The letter with your stamps was put in that
room's mailbox and we waited."

"He never showed?"

"He arrived, all right. With a bang. The bastard set off
a car bomb right in front of the hotel, and in the excitement
someone grabbed the letter from the box and got out

through the back. He outsmarted us, Lyon." There was a pause. "I did my best. I'm sorry."

"I know you did everything you could," Lyon said.

"Got to sign off. They want to do something else to my face."

Lyon held the phone with the humming dial tone in his hand for long moments before he finally replaced it on its mount.

He awoke on the couch after a fitful sleep. He blinked open his eyes to stare painfully at the bright morning sun streaming through the window. He felt a momentary lift at the color of the day, but then the memories of recent events flicked back into his consciousness and flooded him with depression.

She was gone, very possibly dead. Their only slender lead had disappeared when the man in London had taken the stamps.

He could deal with grief; it was this unknown limbo that tore at him. She could be alive, in pain, in need of medical help. . . . He tried not to think of the horror of all the possibilities.

Rocco had failed, and although Lyon did not know all the details of that failure, he was certain his friend had tried everything within his powers to capture the kidnapper or his accomplice.

Lilacs. She had spoken of lilacs on the short tape recording they had received. It was a clue, if only he could think objectively and decipher what she had tried to tell him.

He had slept in his clothes and felt dingy.

He took a longer-than-usual shower, lathering himself twice and alternating hot and cold water. He dressed slowly and went back down to the kitchen to make coffee.

Bea hated lilacs. She hated them so much that last summer she had expunged the last ancient bushes from her garden with the ferocity that she usually employed with her weeding.

It was imperative that he address himself to the problem. He had let his anxiety over her well-being block coherent thought.

Lilacs were a clue. It was either the name or location of something that would lead him to her.

Lyon ran from the breakfast nook and down the stairs into what had once been a recreation room. Years ago Bea had appropriated it as her political office, and it now contained file cabinets, thousands of coded index cards on her constituents, and other political paraphernalia. The room included a complete set of Connecticut phone directories.

He began to leaf through their pages. There was a Lilac Garden and Shrub Service on the Boston Post Road in Old Saybrook. There were several listings of "Lilac" as a proper name, and a Lilac Dry Cleaners in West Hartford. He scrambled for a yellow legal pad and began to make notes.

He would visit each and every Lilac listing in the hope that . . .

No! It was a wasted effort. He tore up the notes, wadded them, and threw them across the room. If the lilac clue were a direct reference, her kidnapper would not have allowed it on the tape.

It had to be something more oblique. But what?

He took the stairs two at a time as he hurried to his book-lined study. He read the brief entry for lilacs in Volume 14 of the *Encyclopaedia Britannica* several times. Lilacs came from Persia. An interesting fact, but he could not make it connect with anything. Persia was now Iran, the Middle East . . . No. Too vague. He slammed the heavy volume shut and threw it on the desk.

He stood before the desk and found that he was hyperventilating. He seemed to rise above himself, and the room, the most familiar of his life, took on an unreal aura. His heart began to pound and he felt a deep, unreasoning fear.

He was having an anxiety attack, a panic reaction, he thought to himself angrily.

He sat down in the deep leather chair and leaned back. He consciously forced his breathing level to return to normal. The room gradually returned to its usual state, and the attack was over.

Their life had been torn asunder, and he wondered if it would ever return to normal. He was exhausted—tired physically and drained emotionally. He longed for the quiet hours they had spent together, and realized that in three days it would be Sunday, normally their most relaxed of days. Under ordinary circumstances they would follow their years-old routine: breakfast of plump western omelets, steaming mugs of coffee, probably freshly ground Kilimanjaro, along with rounds of English muffins. The massive editions of *The New York Times* and the *Hartford Courant* would be spilled over the breakfast-nook table.

He would grab for the funnies from the *Courant* and then read the Sunday *Times* Book Review section. Bea would take the *Times Magazine* section and immediately turn to the crossword puzzle.

She was the only person he knew personally who did the Sunday crossword in ink without the aid of a dictionary.

Every third Sunday or so, the *Times* would print a puns and anagrams puzzle in addition to the crossword, and Bea's eyes would light up with a special animation.

Anagrams!

He careened off the chair and hurried to the desk where he tore a fresh piece of paper from the stack by the side of the typewriter.

Lilacs.

He began to write variations of the word: lailcs, caills, scilla. There didn't seem to be any anagram that made any sense at all, or much less gave him a clue.

He examined the words again and then reached for a

nearby dictionary. Scilla—he turned pages rapidly until he came to the proper entry.

". . . Old World bulbous herbs of the lily family with narrow basal leaves and pink, blue or white racemose flowers."

He stared down at the entry. It didn't seem to help either. What were racemose flowers? Back to the dictionary.

Racemose, *Webster's Collegiate* told him, was ". . . having or growing in the form of a raceme."

A raceme, *Webster's* further informed him, was a form ". . . in which flowers are borne on short stalks of about equal length and equal distance. . . ."

He slammed the dictionary shut.

Bea had composed a message under the most difficult circumstances. Could she have been confused about racemose and meant for him to read it as "racehorse" or even "racetrack"?

There weren't any horse tracks in Connecticut, but there were car and dog tracks.

Was she held prisoner in some isolated and seldom-used track? He shook his head. Too far afield. He was reaching and would have to approach the problem from a different angle.

He inserted fresh paper into the typewriter and began to peck out the exact words Bea had spoken on the tape.

"He picked me up at the shopping center parking lot, Lyon, but I suppose you know that by now. I have not been hurt, and he tells me that he will let me eat after this tape is complete. It would seem prudent for you to do exactly as he says. Please do, Lyon, because I love you and I want to come home to take care of my lilacs."

He read the words again and again. Most of them were expected, mundane, and right for the circumstances. The only thing he was sure of was that for all the reasons Bea might want to return home, it was not because of the lilacs.

The last lilacs at Nutmeg Hill had been torn up by the roots the previous summer by Bea Wentworth.

The clue was in her last spoken line.

Lilacs?

Under the Lilacs was a book by Louisa May Alcott. Bea had always said that she'd loved Alcott when she was a girl. They didn't have a copy in the house; he would have to borrow one from the library.

> Lilacs,
> False Blue,
> White,
> Purple.

He recited the lines aloud. Yes. Amy Lowell. He rummaged through the bookcases again until he came across a volume of Lowell's poems. He flipped through the index and then to the poem, "Lilacs," reading it again and again as he tried to make contact with his wife's thinking.

A line sprang from the page: "Heart-leaves of lilac all over New England."

All over New England! God, some clue!

He closed the volume in disgust and began to pace the room. He paused by the window overlooking the river, and another line of poetry came to him:

> When lilacs last in the dooryard bloom'd.

His mind went blank. He could not connect the line with a poet. Think. It was famous, and he was a former English teacher. He had read it dozens of times. He paced the room again, grasping for the elusive thought that seemed to squirm farther away as he reached for it.

He was trying too hard.

He sat back in the leather chair and tried to remove his

mind from the immediate thought of identification.

Who were Bea's favorite poets? There would be a connection.

When they were first married, it had been Emily Dickinson. God, her poems didn't have names and there were hundreds of them. Had she written anything about lilacs? Probably.

No. Emily Dickinson was for the young, Bea had said. As she had grown and matured, her tastes had changed.

Bea loved Whitman. Walt Whitman.

The line, "When lilacs last in the dooryard bloom'd," was an elegy for Lincoln.

He searched the books for the appropriate volume and, when he found it, nearly dropped it as he searched frantically for the poem.

He read the first stanza aloud.

"When lilacs last in the dooryard bloom'd.
And the great star early droop'd in the western sky in the
    night,
I mourned, and yet shall mourn with ever-returning spring."

He read the remainder of the poem to himself, but before he was through he knew instinctively that the clue lay in the first stanza.

Just as he knew what flavor Bea liked in ice cream and how many sugars she took in her tea, he knew that this first stanza would lead him to her whereabouts.

What was she telling him?

He went back to the book of poetry and carefully typed out the first stanza in capital letters. He began to scan the poetry as if he were a teaching instructor pouring over a seminar's submission.

He underlined "western sky" with a red pencil and wrote "elegy" in the margin. He underlined several other phrases, "I mourn'd," and "When lilacs last in the dooryard bloom'd."

He tilted back his desk chair and looked down at the words and his note.

She had told him where she was.

Why didn't Bea like lilacs? Everyone loved lilacs. He closed his eyes and tried to recall ten thousand conversations.

"They're eerie," she had once said.

He had laughed. "Why in the world do you feel so strongly about a flower?" he had asked.

"They don't fit into my scheme of things in the garden."

"They go with everything."

"They bring back memories that I don't care to recall."

The conversation had taken place only last summer, when they had been sitting on the patio with drinks in hand. A summer sky had crested overhead, and the river sparkled below. It was a perfect New England summer eve, yet her face had wrinkled with displeasure and he had known she was thinking of something unpleasant. When the silence continued, he had said in a low voice, "A penny for—"

"I was thinking of my Aunt Hattie."

"I thought she was a favorite of yours?"

"She was, and that's why the lilacs. I was only fourteen when she died, and that's sort of a super-sensitive age for a young girl. I was broken up because we had been close. At least as close as a teenage girl can be with a woman in her sixties."

He had nodded, knowing it was not time to speak.

"She was buried from that small chapel at Middleburg College. She requested only lilacs, and the place was filled with them. The smell, that sweet, cloying smell. I'll tell you, Wentworth, it drove me bananas. I had to leave the service."

"So now they are the symbol of death for you."

She had smiled at him. "Enough of that," she had said.

He had fixed them another drink and they had eaten bay scallops on the patio, and the next day she had ripped the last remaining lilacs from their garden and they had gone for a balloon ride.

Lyon slammed from his desk chair and jerked to his feet. His heartbeat had increased, and his palms were moist with tension.

His hot air balloon was in the barn. He ran through the French door to the patio, vaulted the stone parapet, and broke into a full run as he approached the barn. He fumbled with the lock, then slipped into the dim interior. He found the switch by the door and flipped it on, and overhead lights illuminated the room.

His flight case was placed neatly on top of the hot air balloon's neatly rolled envelope. He took out the log and flipped the pages until he found the date of the entry last summer which concerned their only flight to the northwest part of the state.

On June 2 of the previous year, they had trucked the balloon to Hampstead in the western part of the state. They had inflated late . . . he ran his finger along the entry and read it:

Inflation at 2 P.M. Flew at 1250 feet. Winds NNW at ten miles per hour. Three-hour flight. Descended at Reckledge Green at 5:10. R. Herbert in chase car.

He reached back into the flight case and pulled out his maps. He spread a geodetic survey map for northwest Connecticut on the envelope and took a quick measure with his fingers. Direct flight from Hampstead to Reckledge was twenty-seven miles. The wind must have remained relatively constant.

He drew a neat line between the two points. He believed that somewhere along these twenty-seven miles, directly beneath or to either side of their line of sight, lay a cemetery where Bea Wentworth was entombed.

Captain Norbert's lips moved as he read the poem. He finished and thrust it impatiently back across the desk. "Where'd you get the jingle, Wentworth? Off the back of a cereal box?"

Lyon half rose in his chair. "That was written by Walt Whitman."

"Prefer Edgar Guest, myself."

"You can't begin to compare . . ." Lyon stopped. This was insanity. He was arguing literary appreciation with a state police captain while Bea might be dead or dying. "I need your men to check all the cemeteries in the area," Lyon said firmly.

"I heard your wife's voice on the tape too. She said she wanted to come home to take care of her lilacs. That's a natural thing for a woman to say."

"She hates them."

"So be it. But from that one sentence you figure that she's a prisoner in a tomb or grave in the northwest part of the state?"

"Somewhere along a twenty-seven-mile line."

"What about to the side?"

"I've checked with the weather bureau. On June the second of last year, flight visibility was eight miles."

"On either side?"

"Of course."

"Do you know how many square miles that is?"

"Approximately."

"Do you know how many cemeteries are in that area?"

"No."

"Well, I worked in that area when I was a young trooper, and I didn't count them either, but there's a lot. Let me give you a history lesson. Not only does every

70

church in that section have a cemetery, but the towns also have them."

"We can hit them all."

"And there's more. That part of the state, before the textile mills opened up in the last century, was filled with small farms. The farms are gone now, but the cemeteries are all over the lot. They're hidden so deep in the woods that you stumble across them only when you go hunting."

"Are you going to help me?"

For the first time since he had known the man, Norbert had the grace to look embarrassed. "How about that batch of lists we gave you? Come up with anything?"

"No," Lyon lied.

"I can't do it, Wentworth. Not on what you've given me. I'd have to call the Litchfield Barracks in on this, and they would laugh me off the force. A poem, for Christ's sake! A grave! It's just not enough information to pull a bunch of men off patrol to tromp through a lot of rotting tombstones. You have to understand, I have paperwork, reports, manpower utilization forms to fill out. I have to be able to justify what I do."

"I'm sure of this."

Norbert shook his head. "I'm sorry. Try and understand."

7

LYON SPREAD THE GEODETIC map across the breakfast room table and thumbtacked it down. He wished Rocco were back; at least he'd have gotten some aid from that quarter. He sighed and bent over the map. There wasn't time to wait for Rocco's return.

He would have to start by himself, but there was too large an area to cover. He would have to eliminate.

He lay a ruler across the map and drew his first line: the approximate heading they had taken on the balloon flight a year ago. Around the balloon's flight course he drew lines to indicate the areas of visibility that day.

The area was huge and included a huge chunk of the state. More elimination.

He would assume that the kidnapper would not hold Bea in a populated area: towns, villages, and the few cities in the area could be ruled out. He drew black circles around the populated districts.

Northwestern Connecticut contains the foothills of the Berkshire Mountains, and large swatches of land include rolling mountains with lake-filled valleys. Working with the map's contour lines, Lyon began to eliminate other portions of land.

He went to work with a magnifying glass to search for

cemeteries and wished that New Englanders did not revere their dead so much.

Lyon let the Datsun idle at the end of the driveway as he waited for the morning mail delivery. The ransom had been paid; instructions as to Bea's whereabouts should have been received or should arrive this morning. If it wasn't in the day's mail, there might be a phone call. Their phone was being monitored by the police, and he would check in with them several times during the day.

He had an inchoate feeling that there would be no instructions. The kidnapper now knew, as he had probably suspected, that there were police waiting when the stamps were dropped off. Bea might already be dead.

He saw the mail jeep in the distance. It stopped at a box down the highway and then slowly began to approach Nutmeg Hill.

Lyon was out of the car and standing by the box as the jeep braked by his side. "Any news, Mr. Wentworth?"

Lyon shook his head and reached for the mail. He quickly sifted through the few letters and found them all to be familiar bills. He waved at the mailman and climbed back into the small station wagon and drove away from Nutmeg Hill. He was a balloonist in heart and soul, and like his counterparts of the sea who depended on sails and hated powerboats, he had an active dislike for fixed-wing aircraft with gasoline engines. There would be no choice today. A small aircraft would be the only way to cover the chunks of territory he had to inspect. A helicopter would be better, but that would require a drive to Hartford to arrange for a rental, and time was too short.

Time. He remembered a harrowing balloon flight several years ago when a quirky downdraft had made his hot air balloon dip dangerously near the towering pylons of a high-tension line. He had immediately activated the pro-

73

pane burner to give lift to the balloon, but a wind had shoved him toward the lethal power line.

The mental calculations consisted of a mental graph: the time available for the balloon to lift as its envelope heated, and the rate of drift toward the power line. In seconds the decision was made and he had leaped out of the gondola. The fall had nearly killed him, but he had remained conscious long enough to see the hot air balloon incinerate itself on the power line.

It was such a convergence of factors that he now felt about Bea. The graph lines were intersecting—today. He pressed down on the accelerator and sped toward the Murphysville Airport.

The town's airport, which consisted of a single runway, had a dozen planes tied down and chocked along its concrete expanse. A hangar and a small operations office made up the remainder of the complex. A wind sock mounted on the top of the hangar hung limp against its pole.

Gary Middletown, the manager, his crushed fifty-mission cap jauntily perched on the rear of his head, smiled at Lyon. "What's up?"

"I'd like to rent a small plane as soon as possible. I want something maneuverable with a low stall speed."

"I've got a Tripacer that's all gassed up and ready to go."

Lyon nodded. "I'll take it."

Gary handed him a form to sign and a ballpoint pen. "Can I see your license?"

Lyon jerked his wallet from his pocket and handed the laminated license across the counter, signed the form, and picked up the small bag he had carried into the building. "The red-and-yellow one midway down the track?"

Gary Middletown shook his head. "Ah—Lyon, this is a hot air balloon license. It's NG for conventional craft."

"My private pilot's license expired years ago. I never flew after I took up ballooning."

74

"Sorry. You'll need a pilot to go with you."

"Fine. Just please hurry," Lyon said impatiently.

"I'm the only pilot here and I have to run the shop. Herb flew a family to the Vineyard and should be back late this afternoon."

"It's a favor, Gary. I need that plane. Now!"

"I can't do that, Lyon. You haven't flown in years and would be rusty as hell. If anything happened to you or the plane, the FAA would close me down."

Lyon looked out the window a moment and then pointed. "You have any of those for rent?"

Gary's gaze followed the pointed finger. "You've got to be kidding! Those are death traps. I keep them here because I need the rental money, but I wouldn't fly one if my life depended on it."

"They don't require a license, do they?"

"Well, no, but do you know how many people were killed in ultralights last year?"

"I'm not interested, Gary. Give me a rental agreement. In fact, now that I think about it, an ultralight will fit my purposes. What's their landing run?"

"Sixty to a hundred feet."

"That will do just fine."

Lyon stood at the far end of the runway looking at the fragile craft in front of him. He shook his head; the damn thing was scary. "What's it called?" he asked Gary Middletown, who was standing slightly to his rear.

"It's a Pterodactyl Ascender."

"Pterodactyl? It sounds like something prehistoric."

"My opinion exactly. You know, Lyon, those are two-cycle engines, and you sit on practically nothing. The flying surfaces are controlled by those wires."

"You don't get any simpler than a hot air balloon. What are the specs on this thing?"

"All right," Gary said tiredly. "You've got a five-gallon

fuel tank with a one-point-five gallon-per-hour consumption. A takeoff roll of one hundred twenty-five feet and a glide ratio of nine to one. What can I tell you? It's a damn hang glider with a thirty-horsepower engine attached. You do any aerobatics and it comes apart at the seams. Stay away from turbulence, if you can, and watch out for wires and mountains. Better yet, don't go up in it."

"Uh-huh." Lyon lashed his small bag of tools to the rear of the seat and began to untie the small craft from its lashings. "Thanks, Gary."

The airport manager shook his head and turned his back to Lyon as he strode back to the small operations building.

Lyon hoped that flying was like riding a bicycle—once you learned, you never really forgot. There was no denying, however, that you were rusty after a decade of pulling propane levers rather than trying to stabilize a hundred-pound piece of wire and cloth in the air.

He revved the engine up to 5,500 RPM, kept it there a moment, and then released the brakes. The ultralight wobbled down the runway and in less than half the length of a football field was airborne.

The right wing dipped precariously and nearly brushed against the runway. Lyon fought to stabilize the craft into some sort of rational flight.

He climbed to what he estimated was a thousand feet and took a northwest heading toward the foothills of the Berkshires gleaming green in the distance.

There was a grace to the flight that he might have enjoyed if his misson had not been so important, and also if the sputtering small engine located only inches from the rear of his head had not been so loud. He missed the silent vertical ascent of his balloon and the sense of oneness with the sky that he had in a drifting balloon.

He stabilized the craft and reached into his shirt where he had stuffed his map with its circled locations.

Lyon reduced the Pterodactyl's speed to 40 miles per hour, its most effective cruising speed. The tiny craft still yawed alarmingly, and he tended to over-correct, but gradually his feel of flying was returning. The craft began to gyrate less and less and and to fly almost normally.

After forty minutes of flight, he spotted the first cemetery circled on his map. He put the craft into a descending pattern and approached from the east. The cemetery loomed larger than his old maps indicated, which meant that it had been enlarged by the acquisition of more land over the years.

The ultralight was nearly at treetop level, and he watched carefully for an access road that would be wide enough for his wingspan.

He realized with a start that there was all sorts of room to land; in fact, the whole cemetery could be considered one large landing field.

There weren't any monuments, crypts, or aboveground markers of any kind.

He reduced his altitude until he was only feet off the ground.

All the markers were brass plates recessed into the ground. There was a small chapel at the far end of the plots, but it looked used, and two groundskeepers on mowers lounged near its entrance.

A gigantic oak tree loomed immediately before him.

Lyon immediately increased the RPM on his small engine and nearly set the ultralight on its side as he tried to slideslip around the massive trunk of the ancient tree.

His right wing was nearly brushing the ground, but the small plane managed to slip past the oak's trunk, and he changed its attitude of attack to fight for height.

One graveyard down. Thirty to go. He felt quite positive that the cemetery he had just checked out would not be suitable for the kidnapper. The small chapel was obviously in use, and there were no crypts removed from sight that would give adequate cover.

He glanced down at his map and adjusted his course for the next circled area.

He thought that perhaps it was the seventh—or was it the eighth?—when it happened.

It was an old cemetery nestled in a cove of trees at the end of a valley. As he made a slow, 30-mile-an-hour approach to the grounds, he could see the small fallen American flags and withered baskets of flowers left over from the Memorial Day ceremonies weeks before. Needlelike monuments and large family crypts were spotted across the overgrown grass of the cemetery, and the land was pitched in a deep incline that would make landing difficult.

He finally saw the rutted dirt road that wound up from a narrow asphalt lane and gradually petered out near the apex of the hill. He banked the ultralight in an easy glide and throttled down to near stall speed as he flew over the dirt road looking for the smoothest portion on which to land.

He set the tricycle landing gear down on the road with a jolt that bounced him half a dozen feet into the air before the plane settled into a landing roll.

The road was narrow—too narrow—and the wings of the plane jutted over its shoulders and barely cleared some of the medium monuments on the side. Lyon knew that he had nearly seven feet of clearance from the ground to the wings, but if any of the larger monuments were near his glide path, the wings would hit and shatter.

A 30-foot-high white marble obelisk, built by some long-forgotten merchant prince, loomed at him not a yard from the shoulder.

He wouldn't make it!

He tried to stop the Pterodactyl, but its landing gear was slithering back and forth on the rough road surface. The monument rushed closer. The plane's wing tip would hit the stone and swing the small craft around, smashing its delicate structure into pieces that would resemble a child's bent toy.

He would survive with a few bad jolts, but the search would be held up for days, until he recovered sufficiently to ply these back roads by time-consuming ground transportation.

In a final act of desperation, he swerved the ultralight and allowed it to careen over the narrow shoulder to the far side of the road, away from the monument. It passed between two rows of weathered tombstones and rocked to a gentle halt by the wire fence of another obelisk.

The Pterodactyl was intact and would fly again—that is, if he could take off on the rutted surface of the dirt road.

Lyon climbed from the narrow seat and unstrapped the small bag of tools from the rear of the seat. Weight had been important, and so his tools were light: a flashlight, a stethoscope, an ice ax with cold chisel, and an army entrenching tool whose blade folded back against the stock.

He began to walk toward an old mausoleum protected by an iron fence whose front gate had half rusted until it canted from its supports. He was thirty feet from the crypt when he heard the sounds faintly echoing from its interior.

"Oh . . . oh God . . . please . . ."

It was a woman's voice. Lyon dropped everything to the ground but the ice ax and the flashlight. He ran at full speed toward the ancient mausoleum. As he drew closer he could see that the metal door was slightly cracked.

Again the voice from the interior. "Oh, Jesus . . ."

He was past the rusted gate now; two more steps and he would be in the mausoleum itself. His shoulder hit the interior metal door and the shock of the impact jolted him, but the door creaked inward and a shaft of light fell across the stone floor.

Lyon flicked on the flashlight and raised the ax. "Let her go!"

Their eyes flickered in the light as they stared up at him.

Lyon slowly lowered the ax and took two backward steps.

"My father sent him!" the girl screamed.

"He's a goddamn pervert," her boyfriend answered. "You seen enough, mister?"

"I . . . I'm sorry," Lyon said. "I thought you would have heard my . . . never mind." He turned and, red-faced, left the crypt and its young lovers.

It was ten minutes later, when he had finished checking out the cemetery and was turning the ultralight around, when the young couple came out of the crypt. She was still adjusting her clothing, and he wheeled a motorcycle around the squat stone building and prepared to kick-start it. He glared at Lyon. "Okay, Peeping Tom. The place is all yours, pervert." The motorcycle roared into life.

Lyon wheeled the ultralight in a semicircle and positioned it for takeoff. It was going to be a long day.

The cemetery was barely visible from the road, and if his map hadn't indicated its location, he might have flown past without landing. The rusted gate was nearly obscured by high weeds, and the graves had not been tended in years. The foundation of a church was nearby, its interior filled with fire-blackened timbers.

Seeing that there was no road within the cemetery itself that would accommodate his craft, he decided on an easy road landing. He throttled the engine back to a near stall and made his approach. It was a bad landing that ran too close to the rusting fence, and the wing almost engaged the iron spikes. He was tiring, and in addition to that, the limits of the craft's cruising range had been reached. There was a small airport near Torrington where he would land and refuel after this last search.

He unstrapped himself from his precarious seat and

pushed the ultralight off the road until its nose touched the cemetery gates. He retrieved his tools from behind the seat and started wearily into the cemetery.

How many had it been? He had lost count. He could take out his map and count off the ones he had searched, but it hardly seemed worth the effort.

It was all too farfetched. Under the stress of her abduction, Bea might have mistakenly named lilacs, or he could have misconstrued the whole clue and missed an obvious answer. . . . All his doubts seemed to merge into his aching body as he trudged up the steep incline of the small country cemetery.

He walked the lanes between the gravestones, keeping an eye open for a possible air vent. Years ago he had read of a kidnapping in the south where a young girl had been entombed in a packing case buried beneath the ground. He sounded the ax against any above-the-ground crypts or mausoleums and listened with his stethoscope for sounds in their interiors.

He walked the leaf-strewn lanes between the stones. The ones located nearest the road were the oldest. Their faces were worn smooth from the elements; only a few with deep-cut letters still announced the name of the deceased. Lyon had a strong sense of history, and now he felt a living presence, as if the souls of those interred were near him.

He was not a spiritualist, nor was he a believer in any facet of the supernatural; still, he felt he could somehow sense the dead.

He was tired and sat on a toppled stone. A soft breeze brushed his face, and he sighed and forced himself back to his feet.

The crypt at the top of the hill stared down at him like a malevolent face. He felt drawn toward it and began to walk up the hill. Etched into a marble slab across the front of the tomb was the family name, Trumbull. It was a vaguely familiar name, yet he couldn't place it.

The tomb was built into the side of the hill, with a marble face broken in the center by a locked barred door before an oval interior metal door.

Lyon inserted the stethoscope earpieces and pressed the bell through the bars until it was flush against the inner door.

With his free hand, he slammed the ax against the metal until sound reverberated through the tomb and across the valley.

He listened for a moment and was about to turn away when he heard a sound that seemed like a faint scratching from within the crypt.

He tore the cold chisel from his back pocket and placed it against the padlock that chained shut the barred door. He struck the chisel with the ax three times before the lock fell apart. He noticed that the fallen lock was not rusted and was by far the newest artifact in this ancient graveyard.

Lyon pulled open the barred door and swung up the lever restraining the interior door. He pushed in the final barrier.

A large rat blinked in the bright light and then scooted between his feet and loped down the hill.

"Damn!" he said. He would have to replace the lock he had just broken. That meant a round-trip to the nearest town. He began to close the door.

The sound was hardly human, a guttural gasp.

Lyon shoved the door open with such force that it banged against the interior wall. Mid-morning sun fell over his shoulder and crept into the tomb.

She stood before him chained to the wall. Her eyes were sunken, with deep rings surrounding their sockets. Her clothing was tattered, and she was coated in dust and grime. Wisps of hair straggled over her face as she squinted painfully into the bright light.

"You took your time, Wentworth," Bea said.

8

HE CARRIED HER DOWN the hill past rows of gravestones toward the road. He had been able to chisel one end of the chain from the ring on the crypt wall, but the handcuff on her right wrist defied his simple tools, and the chain dangled behind them and clanked against stone as he made his way through the rusted gates.

She nuzzled into the hollow of his shoulder. "Tell me this is the real thing," she whispered.

"It is. You're free."

She lifted her head, and the sun, falling through the leaves, dappled her face. She smiled and resumed her position against his neck. "I've lost weight. It makes for easier carrying."

"We'll fatten you up with lots of thick milk shakes and steaks." He knelt with her and let her rest her back against the fence by the road. "A car's bound to be along soon and we'll get a ride to the nearest town."

"I want to go home," she said.

"I think we had better have you checked out at a hospital."

"I just want to go home. I'm tired and that shouldn't be. All I've done the past few days, however long it's been, has been to sleep."

He felt for her wrist and tried to take her pulse. It

seemed fast and erratic. "I want you seen by a doctor before we go home. I'm sorry it took me so long. It took a while to find out what you meant by the lilac clue."

She smiled at him with drowsy eyes. "I knew you'd get it eventually. See, I have complete faith."

"We're lucky you knew where you were. You practically drew me a map."

She yawned. "The only thing I had to go on was the Trumbull name."

"Trumbull?"

"The name of the people whose tomb I inhabited. I knew I was in an old cemetery, and then I saw the family name Trumbull cut into the sarcophagus."

"I still don't understand."

"That's because you aren't a political person. When I ran for secretary of the state, I traveled through all of Connecticut. In the northwest one of my staunchest backers was a Rebecca Trumbull. A sweet old lady whose family had been here since before the Revolution. It's not a common name, and that meant I was probably in her family mausoleum. That balloon trip we took last year had to have passed near here."

"A mile away, as I compute it."

"Did you give him what he wanted?"

"The stamps?"

"Whatever he asked for on the tape. I was so busy thinking about the Trumbulls that I wasn't paying much attention."

"Yes, I did."

"How did we afford it?"

"It's complicated. I'll explain later."

"Then you didn't need the lilacs," she said with another yawn. "He would have told you where I was when he got the ransom."

"I guess," Lyon said. He didn't tell her that the letter containing her location had never arrived. Nor had there been a further tape or phone call. He wondered how and when he could tell her about the sale of Nutmeg Hill.

"I feel funny, Wentworth."

"We're sure to get a ride to the hospital in a few minutes. Can you last that long?"

She laughed with a voice that skirted the edge of hysteria. "Oh, sure. Why not? I've lasted this long and it isn't dark anymore. Did you know that I was afraid of the dark?"

"No, I didn't," he replied softly.

"Well, I am. Never knew it before. I mean, even as a little girl I never cowered under the covers to get away from the monsters. There is a bogeyman, Went. He's out there somewhere. He's lurking in the bushes or behind the rocks and trees or in a van ready to spirit us away to some dark place."

Lyon did not answer.

"He got me. Boy, and how he did. In the beginning he looked at me with a strange sort of lascivious glare. . . . I thought my honor was ready to fall, and I didn't even have a tower to fling myself from." She laughed aloud. "But he didn't. I guess I turned him off, and so my honor remains intact. Pleased to hear that, Wentworth?"

"I'm glad you weren't hurt."

"Hurt? No way. A little chain on the old wrist." She clanked the chain curled at her feet. "Maybe I'll leave it on as a sort of reminder of how vulnerable I am."

Lyon tried to speak, but his throat was tight and swollen, and the words wouldn't come. "It's going to be all right," he was finally able to mutter. "The hospital . . . maybe a shot of something." A pickup clattered down the road toward them. "Maybe we have a ride," Lyon said as he stood to flag down the truck.

"They wouldn't let me see her."

Lyon looked up from his fourth cup of bitter hospital cafeteria coffee to see Rocco Herbert looming over him. He stood and put an arm around his large friend. "Are you all right?"

"A few minor glass wounds in my neck and a bad case of embarrassment over letting the bastard get away." He straddled a chair. "What's with Bea?"

"She seemed all right when I first found her, but became quite depressed by the time we arrived here. They have her under sedation and are trying to balance her fluids and cure a mild case of dehydration."

"Then she's going to be all right?"

"Yes."

"I haven't had time to get the details yet. How in the hell did you find her?"

Lyon told him how Bea managed to indicate her location with the lilac clue."

"One smart lady," Rocco said. "Thank God you got to her in time."

"What happened in London is disappointing. Everyone seemed to be sure you'd grab the guy when he made the pickup."

"He outsmarted us. He did something we weren't prepared for. We had the Hotel Dalton, where the drop was made, covered with the proverbial goddamn blanket. Yard guys all over the place, FBI observers and me watching from across the street with a spotter scope. I saw your letter, with the stamps, put into a room mailbox. I had my scope trained on it when the damn bomb went off."

"You're lucky your eyes weren't hurt by flying glass."

"The Yard guy posing as the room clerk lost an eye. There was someone in the hotel who knew when the bomb was going off and who grabbed the letter from the box and ran."

"And there's no trace of Willingham, the man it was addressed to?"

"We never found a trace of anyone by that name except for the typewritten room-reservation letter."

"We're doing fine, aren't we, Rocco? All the police resources of two continents behind us and the guy gets away with it."

"We're not through. Norbie's people and the FBI are searching the area where you found Bea. They'll turn up something. Has Bea been able to make a statement?"

"No. I talked to her a little, but we didn't go into anything in depth except about the Trumbulls' crypt. She sort of faded out after that."

"When she's rested and can talk, maybe we'll be able to get something to go on from her."

"I came across a name that appears on both the flight manifests and the stamp-journal list. Robert R. Traxis of Wessex."

"Christ! That's the guy who goes ape over Bea's politics."

"The same one."

"Did you tell Norbie?"

"I went to see Traxis myself and found that he has a perfect alibi for the night Bea was taken. He appeared at a town meeting and is identified in the minutes."

"Another strike-out."

"Maybe not completely. He's got a man working for him by the name of Reuven something or other who seems to act as a valet-handyman type of person."

"And you want me to check into him?"

"Very much."

"You conjecture that this fellow Reuven handled the Connecticut end while Traxis made the pickup in London?"

"It's a possibility."

"That's the best lead so far. I'll run it down as soon as I find out what Norbie's up to at the cemetery."

"What happened to my friend?"

The alarmed voice behind them startled them. Lyon jumped, and Rocco's hand automatically brushed against the magnum holstered at his belt.

"Holy Jesus, Kim! Don't sneak up on us like that," Rocco said.

"They told me at the nurses' station you were down here. Any chance of getting a cup of coffee?" Kim Ward plunked into the empty seat at the small table as Lyon went back through the cafeteria line to get her coffee.

For years, Kim Ward had been Bea's close friend, campaign manager, assistant, and had served as deputy secretary of the state when Bea held that office. The two women were alike in many ways: feisty, strong-willed, and always ready to do battle for their beliefs.

Lyon returned to the table with the coffee, and Kim took the cup gratefully.

"You look like hell," Rocco said.

"You always were one with the fast compliment, Herbert. My plane just landed. I can't tell you how many hours . . . or is it days that I've been in the air? I came across a week-old *New York Times* in this crazy African hotel and saw a short article about Bea's kidnapping."

"You flew back from Africa to help?" Lyon asked, although he knew the answer.

"They won't let me see her, Lyon."

"She's under sedation right now."

"What's this Africa bit?" Rocco asked.

"Kim was appointed to a committee formed by the American Friends, to investigate child malnutrition in several countries," Lyon said.

Kim finished her coffee. "As soon as I saw the newspaper, I tried to fly out. I had one hell of a time until I caught a feeder flight to Kenya and a flight to London from there."

"Everyone seems to fly to London these days," Rocco said bitterly.

"Did you finish your report?" Lyon asked.

"Almost. I can get the rest of the data when the other members of the committee return next week. It's not just starvation, Lyon. It's dysentery. In certain areas dysentery is killing half the children under a year. They go into dehydration, and there's just not enough medical treatment." She stared past them toward some unseen place filled with the horrors she had recently witnessed. "Dysentery, for God's sake!"

"Is there a Mr. Wentworth here? Phone call for Mr. Wentworth."

Lyon turned in his seat to see the cafeteria cashier standing by the cash register with a phone receiver in her hand. He hurried to her. "Yes, thank you. Hello."

"This is Perkins on the sixth floor, Mr. Wentworth. You wanted me to call when your wife awoke."

He recognized the brusque and officious voice of the charge nurse on Bea's floor. "Yes, thank you. I didn't think it would be so soon."

"Neither did we. She has enough Valium in her to keep a normal person out for another twelve hours. Frankly, Mr. Wentworth, she is giving us a very difficult time."

"Difficult?"

"She's trying to leave the hospital."

"I'll be right there."

Lyon stood in the doorway to Bea's private room and tried to see her through a maze of orderlies and nurses that were clustered around the bed.

He heard her.

She was hyperventilating in a rasping, throaty wail. He pushed past two orderlies.

Her arms and feet were strapped to the bed frame with heavy leather restraints. She fought against the straps. Her shoulders were arched, raising her head a few inches off the pillow. Her eyes were wide with fright.

"Let her go!" Lyon commanded. He pushed a nurse aside and fumbled at the leather strap pinning her right arm. "Don't you idiots know where she's been? Get these damn things off!"

Hands motivated by his voice of command undid the straps. In seconds Bea was free and swinging her feet off the side of the bed.

"Always to the rescue, Went. Thanks."

Lyon turned to glare at the offending hospital personnel. "Who ordered this?"

"The resident," a nurse answered. "Doctor Panditt felt that because of the amount of Valium we had given her it would be dangerous for her to sign out."

He kissed Bea. "They didn't realize."

"No matter. I'm going home. There's a lot to be done. The garden hasn't been tended in a week or more. I bet you've forgotten to do any shopping. Maybe I'll see my friend at the shopping center parking lot." She laughed in a high-pitched falsetto. "Things to be done. My God, I'm running for majority leader." She pushed away from the bed. "Where are my clothes?"

"In the closet," one of the nurses said.

"I'm calling the chief resident," the charge nurse said.

"Do that," Bea replied. "I'm still signing myself out right now. Where are those clothes?" She opened the closet door and looked in horror at the bundle of dirty clothes she had worn to the hospital. "Oh, God. Gross."

"I haven't had time to bring fresh things," Lyon said. "I think you had better get back in bed."

"No way. I'm leaving. There's too much to do, and I've goofed off long enough."

Lyon looked at his wife and saw the fear that still lurked in her eyes, which seemed filled with dark flecks. He wanted to hold her.

"Get back in bed, honey," Kim said softly from the doorway.

Bea whirled to meet her new oppressor. "You can't . . . Kim!"

"You sure can get in a lot of trouble when I'm not

around," Kim said as she stepped into the room. "Everyone but Lyon out," she commanded.

Lyon stepped back as the nurses and orderlies filed silently from the room and Kim approached Bea. The two friends grasped each other's shoulders and then embraced.

"We're running for majority leader, Kim. We have lots to do."

"I know." Kim hugged Bea tighter. "In a while."

"It was ghastly."

"I know."

For the first time since he had found her, Lyon saw his wife's shoulders heave and her body convulse as she cried in her friend's arms.

He left the room and quietly shut the door.

Lyon felt a wedge of stomach pain as the Murphysville police cruiser pulled to a stop by the rusted gates of the country cemetery. Other vehicles, some with dome lights, others unmarked, lined the quiet road. Roaming state police troopers with downcast eyes marched along the rows of tombstones, searching for anything that might provide a clue to the kidnapper.

Lyon and Rocco trudged up the hill toward the summit where the Trumbull mausoleum squatted. A portable gasoline generator that had been placed outside the vaulted entrance hummed while lights flickered inside the crypt.

Captain Norbert paced up and down before the tomb.

"What are you doing, Norbie?" Rocco asked.

"We don't need civilians at the crime scene, Herbert," Norbert snapped as he waved a deprecating hand at Lyon.

"For Christ's sake, he found the crime scene."

"I don't need any meddling, Rocco. This is state police jurisdiction."

"Knock it off," Rocco mouthed as he walked inside the vault.

Lyon followed Rocco inside. "Why isn't he following us?"

"One of Norbie's quirks. He wouldn't come in here if his life depended on it. In fact, he wouldn't even be in the cemetery if his job didn't demand it."

"A state police officer who's probably pried dozens of cadavers from wrecked cars is afraid of cemeteries?"

Rocco shrugged. "Everyone's got his thing. I discovered mine on the flight to London. I hate airplanes."

The interior of the vault was crowded. Photographs were being taken, men were bagging the remains of food and water tins for evidence, and a fingerprint expert was dusting the whole area.

Lyon looked at the stone platform where Bea had been bound and found that he had to turn away. Suddenly the small room seemed oppressive, and he found himself gasping for breath.

"I give you a thou to one that we don't find anything useful here," Rocco said. "The guy's not going to make that kind of error after he's done everything else so well."

"I think you're right," Lyon said as he bolted for the door. Outside he bent over and retched into the tall grass.

"That's why I don't go into those things," Norbert said with a harsh laugh from behind him. "You know, Wentworth, I guess I have to hand it to you. How in the hell you found this place using some damn jingle gets me. This cemetery isn't even on the maps."

Lyon straightened up. "What did you just say?"

"Even if I had cooperated with you, we wouldn't have searched here. This place isn't on the new maps."

Lyon turned eagerly. "Do you have a copy of the map you're talking about?"

"What difference does it make?"

"Perhaps a great deal. Please," Lyon asked with urgency, "let me see your map."

Mumbling something under his breath about cereal

boxes and luck, Captain Norbert strode down the hill toward his cruiser parked near the front gate. He rummaged through a thin attaché case on the rear seat and silently handed Lyon a map. Lyon spread it out on the car's hood and used Norbert's flashlight to examine the coordinates of the cemetery's location. The area appeared as second-growth timber. He checked the date on the map and found that it had been drawn last year. He refolded it and handed it back to Norbert.

"What's it mean?" the state police captain asked.

"I'm not sure." Lyon looked out across the dark valley toward the foothills of the Berkshire Mountains that rose in the distance. The cemetery had been on his map! "How do they prepare those charts?" he asked aloud.

"Who the hell knows? Aerial photographs, or maybe now they use satellites to take strip photographs. Something like that."

Lyon turned to look out over the small cemetery. The trees had grown in the last few years until they now formed a heavy canopy over the monuments. From the air the whole area would appear wooded, unoccupied by either the living or the dead.

The charts he kept in his flight case atop the hot air balloon were years old. He had been meaning to replace them, but had never gotten around to it. He recalled the constant chore of computing magnetic declination shifts from such old charts as he moved the magnetic north location a certain number of degrees for each year of the chart's age.

The kidnapper had planned each move of his crime with such care that it was doubtful that he would have used maps as old as those in Lyon's flight case. The kidnapper had not used a map to select this particular location.

Lyon ran possibilities through his mind: The kidnapper lived in the region and knew the area well . . . careful men do not foul their own nest, he argued to himself and discarded that line of thought. He had discovered the location accidentally . . . nothing in this matter smacked of chance. It was all well rehearsed and planned. That left a third and final possibility—the abductor knew of the cemetery by another means.

The newer cemeteries were often visited, but this one had been abandoned years ago . . . unless it contained a family plot that held particular significance to one family.

"Can I borrow this flashlight?"

"You on to something?" Norbert snapped.

"I don't know. I just want to look around." He walked along the rows of stones and shone the light on each legible name. He mentally cataloged them as the light flicked over the inscriptions.

He found the pie on the other side of the hill behind the Trumbull mausoleum. It resembled a large triangle, or pie-shaped plot, with a tall monument dominating the apex of the triangle and rows of smaller stones radiating from the base.

The single word "Stockton" was engraved in the base of the largest monument. The last stone on the right, at the rim of the pie, was also the newest. Lyon flicked the light across its face and read:

Bates Stockton
b 1920 d 1960

Lyon had known a Bates Stockton. He had known him well, and knew that the man had reason to hate him and anyone he loved.

The man dressed in surgical greens stood in the hospital corridor outside Bea Wentworth's room. With the end of visiting hours and the final medication distribution, the rhythm of the hospital had slowed.

He knew that Lyon Wentworth, accompanied by a

large police officer, had left the building some time ago. During evening visiting hours he had openly prowled the corridor and had seen no one enter or leave the room with the exception of an occasional nurse.

She was now alone.

He reached under the greens into his pants pocket and withdrew the hypodermic needle filled with succinylcholine chloride. It would be a quick and painless death, a single tremor as muscles ceased to function and the heart went into fibrillation until it stopped. She would be dead seconds after the injection. Then he would run down the corridor and into the stairwell, tearing the greens from his body as he made his way to the first floor and the nearby parking lot where the van waited.

He took a final glance up and down the corridor to ensure that he was alone and then pulled the surgical mask up over his lower face. He opened the door and stepped into the room.

The slightly cracked door allowed a patch of light to fall across the bed while the rest of the room remained in shadows. He watched the slow rise and fall of her chest and knew that she was in a deep sleep. He held the hypodermic before him and gently depressed the plunger until a few drops of liquid trickled from the nose of the needle. He stepped toward the bed.

"Hold it!" A voice from the dark corner shattered the silence of the room. "What do you think you're doing?"

He turned toward the woman in the corner. She had been dozing on a chair as she kept an all-night vigil over her sleeping friend. "Attending's orders," he replied.

"No way, baby." Kim stepped between him and the bed. "My friend has had all the medication she's going to get tonight. Why the mask?"

"Out of the way!" He reached forward to knock her away, but she stepped to the side with a lithe movement and kicked out with her foot, landing a painful blow on his ankle. He involuntarily groaned.

"You've got two seconds to get out of here!" Kim said.

He dropped the hypodermic needle to the floor and simultaneously reached under the greens to grasp a spring-loaded switch knife. He clicked the blade into position. "Out of my way, black bitch!" He lunged toward the bed.

Kim shoved a wheeled nightstand toward him with all her force. The top edge caught him in the abdomen as he clawed for the form on the bed, sending him sprawling backward from his off-balance position. Her foot stamped on his knife hand, and the switchblade slithered across the floor. He turned over and scrambled across the room toward the corner where it lay, but she was quicker and snatched the knife from his reaching fingers.

"Okay, bastard! Come get it!" Kim crouched and held the knife firmly in an upward thrusting manner. "Now we see who does the cutting."

"Black bitch!" he said as he lunged for the door and fled the room.

Kim followed him, but closed Bea's door behind her before she began to scream. "Call security!" she yelled. "Stop him!"

The man in the greens pushed through the swinging doors into the stairwell and took the steps three at a time as he dashed for the lower floor and the parking lot. He cursed the woman on the sixth floor whom he could still hear yelling after him.

9

"ALL RIGHT, YOU GUYS, what's up?" Bea stood before the small mirror over the dresser in the hospital room putting the finishing touches to her appearance. Lyon had brought fresh clothing from the house. She had taken a long hot shower and done her hair, and now she gave a final few brushes to her short-cropped hair as she examined the others in the mirror. "Come on, now. I'm a big girl. I'm nearly all recovered and back with it. What's up?"

"You had a visitor last night," Kim said.

Lyon twitched open the venetian blinds and appeared to be looking at the parking lot in the rear of the hospital with great care.

"He was dressed in a surgical gown and carried a hypodermic needle," Rocco said.

"Filled with what?" Bea's brushing motions stopped, but she watched them closely in the mirror.

"A powerful muscle relaxant," Rocco continued. "Luckily Kim was still in the room and drove him off."

"Which explains why Jamie Martin is sitting in front of my room with a shotgun on his lap and practically followed me into the shower."

"It would be easier for us if you stayed here," Rocco said. "I'm putting you under twenty-four-hour guard, but the house is too remote. There are too many hidden approaches through the woods."

"And the hospital room has one door and one window."

"You would be safer," Rocco said. "Why did he want to kill you now, Bea? He certainly had plenty of opportunity while he held you."

Bea's face turned chalk-white. "Because the last time he saw me he came in without his mask on. Lyon, did you ever get a letter or call as to where I was?"

"No," Lyon replied without turning from the window.

"He thought I would die in there. He intended for me to die in there." Bea sat heavily on the bed.

Rocco took a small pad from his breast pocket and hurriedly turned pages. "Give me his description. We'll put out an APB and then spend the rest of the day going through mug shots."

Bea looked desolate. "I can't." She shook her head. "He was only with me a few minutes, and when he lit the Coleman lantern the bright glow made everything turn hazy for me. I had been in the dark so long that my eyes didn't have time to adjust. He could be a dwarf with flaming red hair, for all that I know."

Lyon let the blinds fall back to their original position. "Except that he doesn't know that. He must have inadvertently forgotten the mask on his last visit and later realized you had seen him."

Kim's eyes widened. "And he left her in there to die. . . ."

"But I didn't die, did I? And now he wants me dead."

"You've got to give us some sort of description, Bea," Rocco insisted.

"I can't give you what I don't have."

"We'll try hypnosis. Sometimes that can help."

"You can't hypnotize out of me something that isn't there. I tell you, I couldn't see anything because of my eyes." Bea started for the door. "I'm going home now. Tell officer Martin to pack up his popgun and follow me to Nutmeg Hill."

They drove to the house in convoy. Rocco's cruiser was first, then the small station wagon, followed by Jamie Martin in another police car. Lyon knew that Rocco's magnum would be unholstered on the seat beside him. Jamie's shotgun would be loaded and cocked.

He hadn't spoken to Bea since they'd begun the drive, and now they were both occupied with their own private thoughts.

Lyon remembered a Bates Stockton Junior fifteen years before. . . .

In those days he had been an associate professor of American Literature at Middleburg College and Bates had been a graduate student in one of his seminars. Lyon was also Bates' faculty adviser.

"You're full of shit, teach," said the voice a decade and a half ago.

Lyon had been standing at the window of his third-floor office looking down at the grassy quadrangle below. They were attacking the ROTC building again. The yard below was filled with several hundred yelling, screaming students carrying placards and flags.

"I said, you're full of it, professor," the voice behind him insisted.

Lyon knew without turning that Bates Stockton was sitting on the edge of his desk in the narrow, cramped office and was probably rumpling a dozen student themes with his body. "I am not a professor," he said quietly. "That is a matter of fact. I will not be called names, and that is a matter of privilege." He momentarily wondered why Bates wasn't in the quadrangle protesting with the others, but that would have been out of character for the insolent graduate student. Lyon turned to face him. "Get off my desk!"

Bates Stockton glared at him a moment and then stood. Both men stood a few feet apart, with their eyes locked. "I have the right to submit an original work of fiction in place of my master's thesis."

"I advise against it," Lyon replied. "Your work in my seminar has shown talent, but it is fragmentary and indicates to me that you are not ready for longer work, much less a novel."

"I've finished the book."

"I know," Lyon said tiredly. "That's why I want you to withdraw it from consideration by the committee."

"Stuff it!" the graduate student said with malice.

Lyon sat at his desk and nodded toward the side chair. Bates glared a moment and then slammed into the chair. Lyon picked up the manuscript enclosed in a typing-paper box and turned a few pages. "You have the right to do an original piece of work or research instead of this."

"I'm submitting my novel."

The chanting voices from outside rose and fell as the crowd rocked back and forth between the military science and the main administration buildings. Lyon wondered if he should take the uncompleted manuscript of his Wobbly book home for safekeeping. "I'm giving you a final opportunity to withdraw this book."

"What have you got against me, Wentworth? That's a damn fine piece of work."

"Yes, it is."

Bates sneered. "Those who can't, teach. That's it, isn't it? Your craven little heart is all tied up because I did something you can't do."

"Take my word for it, withdraw it," Lyon repeated.

"You said it was a fine piece of work."

"Except that you didn't write it."

The room was silent except for the sounds of chanting, milling students outside. "No! No! We won't go!"

"What in the hell are you talking about?"

"I've tried to give you every opportunity."

"This is my work, damn it!" He thumped the box filled with the manuscript.

"The book you call *Master's Watch* was published in 1924 under the title *Night Stars*. It was written by a man named Richardson."

"You're crazy. That was years before I was even born. I've never heard of a book called *Night Stars*.

"Neither have many other people."

"Then where in hell do you get off making that accusation?"

"When I was very young, my father brought a summer place on Great Diamond Island. That's in Casco Bay, outside of Portland, Maine."

"I don't need the travelogue, Wentworth."

"Because it is an island, it's customary when you buy a place to get all the furnishings. There were several bookcases filled with old books circa 1900 to 1930. It rained a lot that summer. I read them all."

"You were a kid."

"I know, and I've read a lot of books since then. But your manuscript haunted me. It was something vaguely familiar that I couldn't quite place. It took me three weeks to come up with it, but would you like a line-by-line comparison?"

Bates blanched. "You do this to me and I lose my draft exemption."

Lyon went back to the window and looked down at the crowd. Campus Security police were now joined by town and state troopers and were driving the students back from the quad. It would start again tomorrow, and both sides would go through the ritual again. He wondered if they heard it in Washington. "I'm sorry about that, Bates. I don't agree with this war any more than the kids down there." He turned to face the graduate student. "But I can't allow a plagiarized work to be accepted."

"I'll be drafted."

"I'm sorry."

The sneer returned. "All right, Wentworth. How much do you want?"

"I beg your pardon?"

"The Stockton fortune may be fading, but Grandma still has a few bucks up the family tree that I might be able to shake loose."

"You're offering me money?"

"To keep your mouth shut, or to be absent when the committee meets. For not doing anything and keeping me out of the damn army."

"I couldn't do that."

"Don't hand me the sanctimonious bit. What's your price? You want a girl? I know a couple of juicy coeds that would be willing to put out for you if I asked them in the right way."

"Get the hell out of my office, Stockton!"

"You're serious."

"You can bet your family tree on it."

"I'll get you, Wentworth. One day, I will ream your ass."

From his study he could see her weeding the garden. She wore a wide floppy hat that mostly obscured her face, faded blue jeans, and one of his old white shirts tied at the midriff. She attacked the weeds ferociously while Jamie Martin stood on the parapet above her with a shotgun cradled in his arms. Martin looked bored.

Lyon turned from the window and continued his search through the stuffed file cabinet. He had once calculated that he was about ten years behind in his filing. Folders, news clippings, and manuscripts were shoved into every nook and cranny of two file cabinets and several boxes. The farther into the depths he progressed, the farther back the years. Finally he reached the area that included the material from his teaching career. He continued until he found a Polaroid of his graduate creative writing class during his last teaching year—the year that Bates Stockton had been in the class.

There were six of them seated around a table smiling into the camera—except for the one nearest the photographer, who was grinning sardonically. He knew instantly that the one in front was Bates.

When Lyon went out on the patio, he found the police shotgun leaning against the stone wall. Jamie Martin was in the garden on his hands and knees as he helped Bea weed.

"If we're attacked, you're going to protect her with a trowel?" Lyon asked.

Jamie flushed. "I almost forgot, Mr. Wentworth." He scrambled back to the patio and snatched up the shotgun. "I like working with growing things."

Lyon nodded and went down the stone steps into the garden. Bea looked up and pushed back her hat. "You've found something?"

"I want you to look at this photograph," he said as he handed her the Polaroid of his seminar group. "Do you recognize anyone?"

Bea squinted at the picture. "The girl in back. I think she came to our house for dinner one night."

"That's Pat Hale. She writes children's plays now."

"Thought she looked familiar."

"Anyone else?"

"I don't think so."

"How about him?" Lyon's finger pointed to Bates.

"Unpleasant-looking young man."

"Could he be the one who took you?"

"I don't know. He could be."

"You're not positive?"

"No. Sorry. I keep telling everyone that I can't be sure. I wish I could be, I really do." She bent forward to strangle a weed. "Want to help?"

"No, thanks." He walked back into the house, flicking the photograph with his finger. It could be, he thought. But then again, so could almost any other male in that general-age category. Bates would have changed from the young man in the photo. He paused in the doorway and yelled back at Bea. "Did he ever speak to you in a normal voice? I mean without using the voicebox?"

"Yes."

"Would you recognize his voice if you heard it again?"

"I don't know. Maybe."

Rocco sat in the study with his feet on Lyon's desk and his hands clasped behind his head.

"So much for our security," Lyon said. "I didn't hear you come in."

"Neither did Jamie. I could have shot the three of you from this window."

"Can you give us more men?"

"Keeping one man here around the clock is a strain on the force. You could help if you did such things as keeping your front door locked."

"It's an old habit. Bea wants to go back to work. I don't know how much longer I can keep her cooped up here."

"She ought to stay low until we catch the bastard."

"That could be next year."

"Methinks I hear a twinge of bitterness."

"I haven't told her about the house yet."

"Oh God. You had better."

"I wanted her to have a few days to recuperate. Is there any news at all?"

"I got the background on the guy who works for Traxis." Rocco pulled a sheet of folded paper from his pocket. "Irwin Reuven . . ."

"Irwin?"

"AKA Chloroform Charlie."

Lyon couldn't keep the excitement from his voice. "Then you do have something?"

Rocco nodded and began to recite the information. "Reuven, Irwin, date of birth May 8, 1952. Born in Hartford and attended Weaver High School. Failed to graduate and joined the army. Did not finish his term of enlistment and was let out on a general discharge. Picked up for assault January 1973; suspected burglary November 1973; car theft 1974. All charges dropped until his arrest in 1975 for assault. He got five to seven for that one."

"Where does Chloroform Charlie come in?"

"Getting to it. Paroled in 1979. Last known address is the Wessex home of Traxis."

"Rocco!"

"Okay. There were a rash of apartment-house burglaries in Hartford before Reuven was picked up. The MO was always the same. A lone woman on an apartment-house elevator. A man in a ski mask with a chloroform-soaked cloth. He knocked the women out and took their bracelets, money, even earrings."

"How did they get him?"

"He was unlucky, or the Hartford police were lucky. An off-duty cop was standing by the elevator door when it opened to reveal Reuven and his latest handiwork. They nabbed him on the spot, complete with ski mask and chloroform."

"And now he works for a man who collects stamps and periodically goes to London."

"And who hates Bea. Reuven's prior is awfully similar to what happened to Bea. The ski mask, the cloth, and the drug. I don't believe in coincidences, Lyon."

"You sound as if you've made up your mind?"

"I nearly have. I'd like to have Bea meet him."

"She says she can't identify him, although hearing his voice might help."

"You know, Lyon, we might be able to turn that around."

"How's that?"

"Bea says she can't make a positive ID, but our friend obviously doesn't know that. I think we should arrange a meeting and play it." Rocco scribbled rapid notes on a pad. "I'll set it up. Two other things: I have some items for you in the trunk of my car, and I want you to come downtown with me to talk to someone who has some very interesting facts."

Lyon followed the large police chief out to the drive and peered into the car trunk when Rocco swung it open. "I don't want those!"

He took two backward steps, as if recoiling from what he had seen in the trunk.

"Be logical. I want one in the bedroom, one in the study, and another in the kitchen." Rocco bent into the trunk and gathered in his arms two shotguns and a magnum pistol. Without waiting for Lyon, he returned to the house and placed the weapons on the study desk. "They are all loaded with the safety on. Most people get hurt with so-called unloaded guns. These are always loaded. Remember that, and you won't get hurt."

"I haven't fired a weapon in years."

"Then it's time you relearned. Do you want to go to the range with me?"

Lyon picked up the magnum pistol. It had a heavy, firm weight. He supported his wrist with his left hand and braced his legs as he aimed the weapon. "Even in the service I could never hit anything with a handgun."

"That's why I brought the shotguns along. Point them in the general direction of the target and you'll get him. As long as he's not too far away. Try not to shoot any of my men, please. I need them all."

"I'll make a valiant attempt."

"Stash them away within easy reach in the rooms I mentioned. That way, as long as you're in the house, you'll only be a few steps away from a weapon."

"I really don't care for them in the house."

"They're tools, nothing more."

"They are designed to kill people."

"If you'd come quail hunting with me someday you'd learn different." Rocco hefted a .12 gauge shotgun and raised it to his shoulder. He tracked a nonexistent flock of birds through the window. "A sharp November day. A bird flushed in front of you climbs into the sky, a quick shot. It's not only exhilarating, they're damn good eating."

Lyon snapped open the chamber of the magnum and twirled it once before snapping it closed. "Ever try and hit a flying bird with this?"

"Impossible."

"A deer, maybe?"

"A miracle shot by the most expert of marksmen."

"What's its use?"

"Right now, it's security for your wife and home."

"Built into a compact killing machine that can be carried on one's person."

"I'd hate to have to carry an M-15 around with me all day."

"You're a cop."

"And we carry weapons. At least in this country we do. Do you know that in London the bobbies still aren't armed? The guys with me had weapons on the stakeout, but they had to sign them out."

Lyon hefted the magnum again. "How many like this are there in this town?"

"Handguns? A thousand, maybe a few more or less. I have permits out for a hundred, but most people don't have permits."

"How many burglars did they shoot in the last few years?"

"None. Before you ask, the local statistics are one husband, one wife, and one lover. Burglars, nothing."

"Bea tries. Every session she introduces a revised handgun bill, and every year she goes down in glorious defeat."

"Okay, all ready. I'll tell Jamie we're going downtown for a few minutes. There's someone I want you to talk to."

Raymond Brohl ran his office like a kingdom. His desk was highly polished, clear of all objects except for the time-stamp machine, and he brooked no nonsense in the Murphysville town clerk's office. He had been town clerk for over thirty years, and although it was an elective office, he was seldom opposed.

Unlike most states, Connecticut has virtually no county government and files its land records by individual towns. The large walk-in vault located a few feet from Brohl's desk contained the history of a town; not only its land records, but probate proceedings, vital statistics, and other records. They were all known to Raymond Brohl. He frowned when Rocco and Lyon entered the office.

"I want to speak with you, Raymond," Rocco said.

Brohl turned away from the police chief to finish his conversation with a young lawyer standing stiffly by the side of his desk. "Do you really want to record these instruments in this order, Counselor?"

"Our senior partner just closed the transaction, and he told me to rush them down here for recording."

"Like this?" Raymond Brohl waved a sheaf of legal instruments in the air. His white-haired assistant across the room rolled her eyes appropriately. "Don't they teach you anything at Yale Law School, young man?"

"Well, not about recording documents, Mr. Brohl."

The town clerk continued his lesson in a singsong, pedantic voice. "To begin with, we record the satisfaction of the existing mortgage first, then the new deed, then the new mortgage, and finally the new second mortgage. Doesn't that make sense?"

"Yes, sir. I guess it does. Suppose we do it that way," the flushed lawyer said.

"My idea exactly," Brohl said as he ran the papers

through the date stamps and began to record their receipt in the Day Book with a flowery Spencerian hand.

Rocco nudged Lyon in the ribs and they left the clerk's office.

"You brought me down here to see Brohl chew out some neophyte attorney?" Lyon asked.

Rocco glanced at his watch. "I just noticed that it's Raymond's coffee-break time. In exactly four minutes he will have coffee at May's."

Every small town in America has a May's. They are undistinguished establishments similar only in that they are located near the center of town, have at least one large circular table known as the "coffee table" to the regulars, and provide an unending stream of strong coffee to the local business people.

Raymond Brohl arrived at exactly two minutes past ten and would stay until ten-thirty. He would dispense free information to any of the regulars who asked, expecting nothing in return for his encyclopedic knowledge of the physical facts concerning the town of Murphysville.

"I got a new listing on Elm Street, Mr. Brohl," Darlimple the real estate broker announced. "Number 219."

"House across the street went two years ago for seventy-one five, the next block up had one last month that sold for seventy-six, but they had an in-the-ground pool. List it at seventy-five and go to contract at seventy-one."

Nods were thanks, and Brohl basked in the approval of his peers, which ensured his reelection.

"Tell Lyon what you told me, Raymond," Rocco said.

"Man came in to see me about your place, Wentworth. I gave him the pertinent facts—zoning, engineers' reports, and so on. When I recorded his deed from his corporation, it came back to mind."

Lyon looked puzzled. "Everyone knows that. I sold my place to a builder from Middleburg who is going to put up some condos."

"Of course I know that," Raymond bristled. "Fifty condominiums at two hundred thousand a unit. Real quality stuff."

"What do you estimate, after seeing his plans, and including roads and services, that the whole package will cost to build?" Rocco asked.

"Five mil including the price of the land."

Lyon did a hasty mental calculation. "Can he really get fifty units on this rocky land?"

"If he clusters them he can."

"That brings the total sales price to ten million."

"At a cost of half that," Rocco added.

"Mr. Brohl," Lyon asked, "exactly when did this man first make contact with you regarding my property?"

"A month ago. A month ago Tuesday."

"And his name was Burt Winthrop?"

"Same fella."

Lyon found Bea in the breakfast nook with a sketch pad. She had already filled two pages with detailed drawings and was looking intently at the third, with her pencil clenched between her teeth.

"What are you doing?"

"You remember my telling you about redoing Nutmeg Hill? All those hours in that . . . in that place, that planning kept my sanity. I thought we'd start with the kitchen. You know, if we knock out that far wall, we can use that extra flue we boarded over. I thought we'd turn this into a real country kitchen. Look at what I've come up with so far." She pushed the drawings toward Lyon.

Lyon couldn't look at them and turned away.

"What's the matter?" she asked.

"You know what happened in London?"

"The guy got away."

"With the stamps."

"I don't understand."

110

"There was no other way to raise the money."

Her pencil snapped. "Funny how the human mind can compartmentalize unpleasantries if it tries hard enough. I didn't want to ask. I forced myself to forget to ask. I didn't want to know."

"I had to sell Nutmeg Hill."

She turned to look out the window for a long moment before she spoke. "How long do we have?"

"Another couple of weeks."

She wadded her drawings and bustled from the breakfast nook. "Well then, we have to get going. There's one hell of a lot of packing to do."

"I'm sorry, Bea."

"Not your fault, Went." She turned to face him with tears in her eyes. "Not anyone's fault."

10

"I've described Burt Winthrop to Bea, and she says no way," Lyon said over the phone.

"I never figured it for Burt himself. It's his twin sons I wonder about."

"How old are they?"

"About mid-twenties, I should guess. Taller than their daddy and real hell-raisers."

"Why would he take the gamble? Just to get his hands on a piece of real estate?"

"With a profit throw-off of five million dollars. A lot of men will do a great deal for that sort of money."

"You know, Rocco, at the beginning of each legislative session Bea automatically files a financial disclosure statement. It's not required, but she does it voluntarily. Anyone taking the trouble to check would know our complete financial picture."

"And that you couldn't raise ransom money without selling your real estate."

"Exactly. I still wonder about our friends in Wessex. You're the one who said he didn't believe in coincidences, and Reuven's the one who chloroforms women."

"I'm in the process of setting it up so that Bea can see Reuven and the Winthrops in a protected situation."

"Thanks, Rocco." The phone went dead, and Lyon

continued staring out the window. He picked up a ballpoint pen and began to doodle on a pad, listing Robert Traxis first. The man disliked Bea with a passion, made trips to London, collected stamps, and had an associate with an inclination toward the use of chloroform. Lyon drew heavy lines under the name.

Burt Winthrop, builder and professional country boy, had exhibited an interest in their property weeks before Bea's abduction. Rocco had just indicated that Burt had young sons who had the agility and speed to have taken Bea and then snatched the stamps from under the nose of the London police.

Then there was the Stockton cemetery pie located only yards from where Bea had been imprisoned. What had happened to Bates Stockton after his dismissal from the university?

Lyon reached for the telephone and dialed the one organization he sometimes considered the best skip tracer in the whole country: the Middleburg Alumni Fund Raising Office.

An officious voice informed him that mail for Bates Stockton had been forwarded to a Fernwick address for the past decade. No change of address had been received, nor had mail been returned.

He made a note of the address and went to tell Bea that he was going out.

The borough of Fernwick was theoretically within the town limits of Lantern City, Connecticut, but it actually belonged to a different world. Granted town-within-a-town status through some obscure state law in the late nineteenth century and surrounded by a high stone wall, it had always been an exclusive enclave for the very rich.

Lyon was forced to slow to a halt at the electronically controlled gates that were the only entrance to Fernwick. He waited behind the wheel as a smartly uniformed se-

113

curity guard with a revolver on his hip sauntered over to the car. Lyon knew from map study and past balloon flights over the area that the settlement was built on a peninsula that jutted out into Long Island Sound.

The guard's smile was obsequious but held an underlying firmness. "Can I help you, sir?"

Slowly revolving television monitors were mounted on each gatepost.

"Do you wish to see someone?" the guard pressed.

"Yes. Mrs. Stockton. Please inform her that Mr. Wentworth is here." He made the statement as matter-of-fact as possible, hoping that a direct approach might work.

The guard went into the gate house, telephoned, and returned to the car as the gates swung open. "She is expecting you, sir. Are you familiar with the house? It's the second back from the seawall."

Lyon gave what he hoped was an imperious nod and drove through the gates, which immediately closed behind him. This was old New England money; the houses were unostentatious, rambling, wooden Victorian affairs built at the turn of the century. Wide screened porches ran along their fronts, and each of the so-called cottages was separated from its neighbor by neatly lined shrubbery.

He parked in the driveway of the second house from the seawall. An old woman in a long black dress buttoned to the neck stood just back from the screen door leading onto her veranda. She smiled as he approached.

"Mr. Wentworth, how good of you to come." A delicate hand with finely lined blue veins crisscrossing its surface was extended.

"Thank you," Lyon answered.

"We shall have tea out here if you would like." She sat on a small wicker divan placed behind an ornate silver tea service. "Lemon or sugar?"

"Lemon, please," Lyon said as he sat on a wicker easy chair on the other side of the tea service.

114

She poured with a special care that Lyon imagined had been learned at some long-ago finishing school.

"Did you have a good trip down from the city?" she asked.

Lyon accepted a cup and balanced it on his knee. "Yes, thank you. It was a pleasant drive." He tried to place her age, but the aging process had seemingly ceased years ago; she could be in her mid-seventies or ninety.

She took a dainty sip from a bone china cup and gave a quiet laugh. "I know you must have legal papers in the car, but let us pass the time of day for a few minutes before we go into all those complicated things."

"Ah, Mrs. Stockton, I am perhaps not who you think I am."

"Mr. Wentworth from the law firm."

"No. Mr. Wentworth from Murphysville. I came to see you about Bates Stockton."

She looked past and through him into some distant time and place. "Bates has been dead for many years. Sometimes I forget that."

"I speak of Bates Junior."

"My grandson?"

"Yes, I would judge so. Do you know where he is?"

She put her teacup down. "Bates was never the same after that awful man at the university told those terrible lies about him. I wanted to bring suit, of course, but Bates wouldn't hear of it. He said he didn't want the Stockton name dragged through an awful court proceeding. A very thoughtful boy."

"Does he live here?"

"Oh, goodness no. He did stay with me after his father died. He stayed here until he went to college. He would often sit out here with me at twilight while we had tea together. I would knit and he would play with his things. I've kept all his things in his room, just as he left it. He had a dreadful time in Viet Nam, but of course everyone knows that."

"No, I didn't know. Did you see him after he was discharged?"

"He did stay here awhile, but he smoked those funny cigarettes and took too much medication. I thought it best that he should leave and find his own place."

"Do you have any idea where he went?"

"Yes. I think he went west. Yes, that's it, west to San Francisco. That's where he died, you know."

"Died?"

"They said he took too much medication."

"OD'd?"

"Yes, an overdose of his medication. Poor boy. Such a pity. It was all due to that horrid teacher at the university. We can only hope and pray that evil men like that will have their just rewards in the hereafter."

"I hope so," Lyon agreed.

"Are you sure you don't have any papers in the car for me? They always have so many things for me to sign when they come down from the city."

"I'm afraid not," Lyon replied. He stood. "Thank you for the tea. I must go now."

"Such a short visit. Do come again." Her hand was extended.

As Lyon left the porch, he had a quick glimpse through the open front door into the interior of the house. The cottage had remained unchanged for decades. Immediately inside the front door was a polished Hepplewhite table with a silver calling-card tray containing a small address book next to the telephone. The floors were dull, as if they had not been polished in years. As he walked to the car, the elderly Mrs. Stockton carried her tea service into the house.

Lyon swung the car door open. She had acted senile, and yet she had seemed to have immediate recall of a

116

number of subjects. He had the inchoate feeling that she was not exactly as she appeared.

He turned and hurried back to the porch. The front screen door was closed, but the inner door was still open. The old lady was standing by the phone preparing to dial. He pressed against the house wall and held his breath to listen better.

He heard the dialing and then a connection.

"Bates," she said in a firm voice devoid of any of the frailty she had exhibited earlier, "that awful man Wentworth was here. He was asking about you. . . . I told him you were dead, of course. . . . In San Francisco, dead from drugs. I thought you should know."

Lyon heard the receiver being replaced in the cradle and then steps clacking down the long hall that would lead to the kitchen at the rear of the house. He judged her to be meticulous and guessed that she would tidy the tea service, wash the cups, and replace them in the pantry. He had seconds to do what was necessary.

He slowly levered the screen door open, hoping it would not creak, and then slipped into the dim center hall of the old house. A step to the Hepplewhite table and his fingers closed over the small red-bound address book. He flipped quickly through the pages and saw the end of a life reflected there. Entry after entry had been neatly lined out with blue ink as the old lady's friends and relations had died.

Near the rear of the book was a single entry, Bates, and a phone number: 388-3882.

He shut the book, replaced it, and slipped from the house. The old woman's dialing of the number had taken only seconds; he could assume that meant she had not dialed an area code and that Bates was at a Connecticut address.

*   *   *

Bea Wentworth, with binoculars pressed to her eyes, stood on the cusp of the hill overlooking the valley. Her head turned as she let her field of vision sweep across the complete area below. The trees on the hillside upon which she stood marched in uneven lines down the slope toward the valley floor, but stopped abruptly as the land flattened. The ground below had been ravaged by dozer and back hoe until only red furrows of soil broken occasionally by yawning house excavations pockmarked the land.

She lowered the glasses. "It takes talent to take a nice spot like this and screw it up."

Kim, by her side, nodded agreement. "It's cheaper to take everything down, build the houses, and then plant a few twigs and charge the owners for landscaping."

Bea looked down at her feet and saw the long shadow of the man standing behind her. Jamie's shadow was elongated by the mid-afternoon sun, but the outline of the shotgun on his hip was clearly visible. "Do you have to breathe down my neck, Jamie?"

"The chief said for me to stick near, Mrs. Wentworth."

Kim smiled. "What does he do when you go . . . when you have to . . .?"

"He stands right outside the door," Bea answered. She glanced over to the side, where Rocco and Lyon were in a deep conversation of some sort. Below them, a battered pickup truck swerved off the highway and raised a trail of dust as it sped across the unfinished access road to the development. Bea raised the binoculars and followed the truck as it stopped in front of a weather-beaten trailer sitting on concrete blocks. She saw a dumpy man leap from the truck and storm into the trailer. "Winthrop's arrived," she said over her shoulder.

Lyon nodded. "Did you find out anything, Kim?"

"Sure. Winthrop and sons are in big trouble with this development. He misjudged the local market, his construction loan is at the highest rate of interest, and the debt load must be killing him. He's had the models up for sale at seventy-two five, and there're only five bonds for deeds recorded."

"There could be other contracts not recorded," Lyon said.

"Sure. Double the number if you want, but he's still in trouble."

"Then why would he want Nutmeg Hill for condos?" Bea asked.

"To save his ass," Kim replied. "Your land is a prime location, and he'll sell out with his first model and then use the construction money on that job to relieve some of the debt load on this dog."

"That's a violation of the law," Rocco said.

"So tell me, big chief, who's going to find out, the way he'll phony his invoices? Paying off one job with the loan proceeds of another is done all the time by builders."

"Is it possible that if he doesn't build on Nutmeg Hill he'll go under?" Lyon asked.

"Who can tell for sure?" Kim replied. "Winthrop and Sons are a privately held corporation and their books aren't open, but no matter how you look at it, this job is killing them."

"I think we had best go down there and talk to Burt," Rocco said.

The line of three cars—a police cruiser, the Wentworths' Datsun, and Kim's convertible—wound their way down from the ridge to Boulder Drive and along the cove until they arrived at a large billboard placed by the entrance to the access road.

"Winthrop Acres, pleasure living in Pleasure Valley," Lyon read aloud.

"I know this place," Bea said. "He could have built in a different fashion and still retained the beauty of the land."

"At a higher cost per unit," Lyon answered as he turned and bumped across the dirt road toward the trailer.

Bea jumped from the car when they reached the trailer and strode toward the entrance.

The door opened, and Burt Winthrop stepped down to the ground with a broad smile on his face as he walked toward Bea. "Hello there, pretty lady. Salesmen are all out for coffee, but I'll be glad to show you around." He glanced at the police cruiser parked behind the Datsun and then at Jamie Martin hurrying toward Bea. "What's going on?"

Bea stuck out her hand, and her best political smile creased her face. "I'm Bea Wentworth. I just wanted to meet the man who stole my house."

Winthrop's manner instantly changed as the sales smile metamorphosed into calculating appraisal that almost as quickly changed into the benign humor of the country boy. "You got me wrong, lady. I was helping your husband out of a tight situation. Believe you me, it was moving mountains to come up with so much cash on a day's notice."

"More like thirty days' notice, from what we've learned."

"What are you talking about, sister?"

Lyon came up behind his wife and put a restraining hand on her arm. "You seem to have had an inordinate interest in our property for some time," he said.

"I'm always interested in a lot of property. That happens to be my business. All right, you've had your say. Now leave!"

Rocco approached them. "We would have more words with you, Burt."

"Listen, Herbert, you and your rifle-carrying friend there get off my land. This property is in Middleburg, not Murphysville. You got no jurisdiction here."

Rocco sighed. "That could be arranged."

"Sure it could. I know how these things work. The lady here has political clout. Her husband made a bad deal and now they want out. The aging preppie should have known better."

Bea glanced sideways at Lyon's lanky figure. His sandy hair was rumpled, and a forelock stuck out over his forehead as usual. He wore boat shoes, no socks, khaki work pants, and a polo shirt. My God, she thought, he's been shopping by himself again.

There were shouts from around the corner of a partially completed unit a hundred yards beyond the trailer. A man of Lyon's age scurried around the foundation dressed in a business suit with the jacket open and flapping in the wind as he ran. He saw the police officers and instantly changed his trajectory.

Two younger men rounded the building in full pursuit after their prey. They wore work clothes and heavy boots.

"What in the hell is going on?" Rocco said.

Winthrop smiled. "My boys are talking to the local union representative."

"Call them freaks off me, you old bastard!" the man in the suit said as he reached the trailer and collapsed on its step.

"Now, Harold," the builder said. "You know you aren't supposed to be out here on the job talking to my men."

"I have a right."

The younger men arrived at the trailer and skidded to a stop when they saw Rocco and Jamie Martin.

"These are my boys," Winthrop said. "Rob and Roy."

"We were just running him off," Rob said. "We weren't going to hurt him. No need to call the cops."

"They're just leaving."

Lyon whispered into Bea's ear. "What do you think? Could it be one of the younger ones?"

Bea looked at the two men. They were identical twins. "I think I am more confused than ever," she said.

11

NAKED, LYON WALKED across the bedroom to stand in the cool breeze by the window. He involuntarily shivered and then leaned forward to rest his arms on the sill. It wasn't over. The lines of hurt and unrest caused by Bea's abduction were still rippling outward.

"Lyon," she said in a quiet voice, "come back to bed."

"I couldn't sleep."

"I'll really try this time."

A faint sliver of night glow made her face a white blur on the pillow. "Are you sure he didn't touch you?"

"He didn't try and make love to me. No, that's the wrong way to say it. He didn't try to screw me. Maybe it doesn't make any difference if he did or didn't. He took part of my life and I was very frightened."

"I know you were." He sat on the edge of the bed and pulled her toward him. "God! I should have gotten there sooner."

Her hands bracketed his face. "You know, Went, of all the people in the world, you're probably the only one who could have found me with what you had to work with."

Lyon had a vivid picture of Captain Norbert and their short but bitter argument over the poetry of Whitman versus Edgar Guest. He chuckled. "You know, you may be right."

"Give me time and I'll feel better. You know that I love you."

"I know." He gently pushed her back on the pillow and pulled a light blanket over her slight form. "I have a meeting with some phone books in your workroom," he said. "Go to sleep."

Within minutes he had discovered that the telephone exchange 388 was for the town of Eastbrook on the shoreline. The remaining digits would take longer to locate, but luckily the town was small and the task would not be impossible.

Lyon began to run his fingers down all the listings for Eastbrook.

Midway through the short directory he found the number, which was listed to a B. Notkcots. It took him several seconds to realize that Notkcots was an exact reversal of Stockton. Bates was alive in Eastbrook, and they would visit him in the morning.

He tapped his fingers on the cluttered table. He needed other information also. He wondered if it was too late to call Kim.

He walked upstairs to the kitchen and poured coffee beans into the grinder. He started the small machine and soon the aromatic smell of freshly ground coffee filled the room. It was very late, but what the hell, he thought as he flipped the kitchen phone from its cradle. What are friends for?

He dialed Kim's number and hoped she wouldn't be too grumpy.

The house in Eastbrook was a chipped, dingy, white two-story frame dwelling that abutted the railroad tracks. Lyon turned into the washed-out gravel drive and switched off the ignition, then sat with Bea looking at the bleak house a few yards away.

Although the day had begun to warm under a bright morning sun, the house's windows were tightly shut with drawn shades. The shade on the right upper window was ripped and hung from its roller by one edge, canting downward at a sharp angle. The wood on the narrow front porch was rotted and had collapsed in places, leaving jagged holes. The grass was overgrown, and a broken washing machine sat stoically by the front door.

"I thought you said he came from an old New England family?" Bea asked.

"He does. His grandmother has one of those so-called cottages in Fernwick."

"She's not very generous with her progeny then. This place looks like a New England version of Tobacco Road."

Lyon got out of the car. "Well, better now than later." He walked gingerly across the overgrown lawn and rotting porch, pushed the doorbell and found it inoperable, and finally banged loudly on the door frame.

"Martin and Rocco are going to be mad as hell that we came out without our bodyguard," Bea said.

"I think we're safe in broad daylight." He banged louder. "I didn't think that being followed by a police officer carrying a shotgun would be an inducement for a productive interview." He knocked again.

"No one is home, Lyon."

He glanced over his shoulder at the empty yard. "No car. He could have left after his grandmother's call."

"I think it's a pretty farfetched relationship. What happened between you and a grad student was fifteen years ago. If he harbored any resentment he would have done something before now."

"Maybe."

"Come on, let's go."

"If he's left permanently, there would be evidence to that effect. Clothing would be missing, and valuable items gone. I'm going inside."

"You can't do that. It's called breaking and entering, trespassing, and I don't know what else."

"Let's see." He reached for the door handle. It was unlocked, and the door creaked inward.

The house was bisected by an extremely narrow hall that ran its length and ended at a rear door. Four doors led off the hall. Lyon stepped inside. "Hello! Anyone home?"

"They've obviously left," Bea said, after waiting a few seconds for a response.

"Maybe." Lyon started down the hall. The first door to the right led into the living room. A shag rug covered the floor. The room was devoid of furniture except for a low teak table in the center of the room directly underneath a Depression glass hanging lamp. Throw pillows were strewn around the carpet.

On the left, a double arch led into the dining room, which contained a card table and four folding chairs. He stopped before a closed door and gently pushed it open to reveal a small room filled with books piled on boards stretched across cement blocks. A small unfinished desk was placed by the window.

The kitchen ran the length of the back of the house. Its fixtures were old: a footed sink, a gas stove with the oven above the burners, and a heavy wooden table in the center of the room.

"Anyone home?"

At first he mistook the sound to be a small kitten's mewing. It came from under the table. He squatted and pushed aside one of the wooden chairs.

She wore a rumpled terry-cloth robe and lay in a curled position beneath the table. Her elbows were pulled tightly against her body and her hands covered her face.

"Are you all right?" He reached for her, and she jerked away from his grasp.

"Go away," she said in a barely audible voice.

"Let me help you."

"Please go away."

"What is it?" Bea asked as she arrived in the kitchen.

"There's a woman under here. I think she's hurt." Bea's hand gently pulled at his shoulder. He moved away, and she took his place.

"Come," Bea said in a voice that was compassionate yet firm. "Come now." She tugged on the edge of the robe, and the woman gradually moved toward her. She put her hands under the woman's shoulders and helped her to stand.

The woman clutched the side of the table with both hands as she hunched forward and groaned.

The robe fell open, and they could see that she was wearing nothing underneath and that her thighs and stomach were laced with red welts. "My God!" Lyon said.

Bea glanced at him sharply in a gesture for silence as she put her arms around the woman's shoulders. The woman groaned again.

Her face was haunted. There were dark rims under her eyes, and the left one was blackened in a dark bruise that covered half her cheek. Her long hair hung down in wispy strands.

"Are you Bates' wife?" Bea asked gently.

The woman shook her head.

"His girlfriend?"

The woman laughed abruptly, and then her body jerked as she clutched her side. Lyon realized that she probably had a fractured rib. "Friend? Do I look like a friend? I'm his woman, his old lady, his roommate. Not his friend."

"He did this to you?"

"I fell down the stairs." Again the short laugh, which ended in a grimace of pain.

Lyon retreated across the room and pulled himself onto the kitchen counter, where he silently watched his wife talk to the battered woman.

"Not the stairs," Bea said. "He punched you and then he hit you with something. Something like a belt."

"A harness. Where in the hell did he find a piece of horse harness? It hurt like hell."

"Where did he go?"

She turned to face Bea with fright in her eyes. "Please go. If he comes back while you're still here, it will only make it worse for me."

"Honey, if it gets any worse you'll be dead," Bea said gently. "Would you make some coffee?" she said to Lyon.

Lyon searched through the wide wooden cabinets surrounding the sink and found a half-empty jar of instant coffee. He grimaced at the thought of what it would taste like, but it would have to do. He turned a porcelain knob on the gas stove, and a burner popped lit.

"Why did he do it?" Bea asked.

"I don't know. He just does it sometimes. He's usually very gentle. He writes poetry, you know. I can show you some of it." She half rose from the chair.

Bea put a hand on her shoulder. "Perhaps later."

Lyon handed them coffee.

"He takes some sort of pills to keep him calm. I think that's his problem, you know. He's okay if he stays off the booze, but if he drinks with those pills in him he kinda goes insane."

"And no specific reason for the beating?"

"He goes into a rage about some man called Rentwroth, or Wendforth, something like that. I think he's really hitting him."

"Wentworth?" Bea asked. "Is that the name?"

"Yes, that's it."

"When will Bates come home?" Lyon asked.

"I don't know. Sometimes he's gone for hours, sometimes for days. I can never tell."

"You have to leave," Bea said.

"I can't. He always finds me. Last year I left and went to my sister's, and he found me. He hit me, and he hit her."

Bea sat down next to the battered woman and glanced at Lyon to signal for him to leave the room.

Lyon walked through the house feeling like an alien. There was something unconscionable and obscene in searching through someone's dwelling. He disliked the invasion of privacy, but his compunctions were not so profound as to make him stop.

There were three square bedrooms on the second floor, each room shut off from the sun and lit with a brownish glow through faded shades. The front bedroom was the one obviously in use. A large box-spring mattress had been placed in the center of the room; the only bedding was a tattered sleeping bag. An old bureau and a straight chair completed the furnishings. He opened the closet door and found it filled with men's and women's clothing. He checked the bureau and found men's socks and underwear. It seemed obvious that Bates had left only temporarily and did not intend to stay long.

One of the other bedrooms was empty, while the third was filled with cartons and miscellaneous pieces of furniture piled haphazardly. Lyon walked back downstairs to the room filled with books.

The stamp albums were aligned neatly on the middle shelf. He flipped through one of the bound volumes, noting that it was the work of a serious collector who had been involved for many years. He replaced the volume in its place and sat down in the captain's chair behind the small desk.

He stretched out his arms and locked his fingers together. A desk lamp placed to the side hung over a half-empty box of typewriter paper. The typewriter that had once occupied the center of the desk was missing.

The machine could have been pawned, taken to the shop for repairs, or it could have been destroyed.

Lost in thought, Lyon sat another ten minutes before

he left the study and returned to the kitchen. Bea had her arm around the girl.

"We're going to a women's shelter," Bea said.

"Is that what she wants?"

The girl nodded her head violently.

"I'll help her pack some things and then let's get out of here—fast," Bea said.

Kim sat Indian-fashion on the floor while Rocco sprawled across the leather easy chair. Bea stood by the door as Lyon took his place in front of the blackboard he had trundled into his study.

"If you scratch chalk, Wentworth, I'm leaving," Kim said.

Lyon smiled wryly over his shoulder and then drew three columns on the board, which he labeled Stockton, Burt Winthrop, and Traxis.

"How about a fourth column labeled 'Other'?" Rocco suggested.

"I'm going to restrict this to what we have." Lyon wrote "motive" in each of the columns. He stepped back from the board and folded his arms. "Bates Stockton has held a deep resentment toward me since he was a student of mine."

"He waited a long time," Bea said. "That happened years ago, and why come after me?"

"I can't account for the long wait," Lyon said, "unless his life has deteriorated over the years and I became a symbol of his troubles. In Bates' case, I think he would have abducted Bea because I might recognize him. I think he fully intended to release her until he made the mistake of allowing her to see him without the mask. If revenge were his motive, it would be accomplished by harming my wife and hurting me financially."

129

"Which would account for the disguised voice," Rocco added.

"I did the rundown on his family that you asked for," Kim said. "The once noble Stockton family is wealthy no more. They are in hock up to their eyeballs."

"What about that mansion the grandmother lives in?" Lyon asked. "That's expensive property out there."

"It was put up for sale two years ago, and the Fernwick Association, composed of all the property holders there, purchased it. They let old Mrs. Stockton live there as a life tenant. Rich folks do that sort of thing occasionally."

"Anything on Bates?"

"Lousy credit rating because of bounced checks, and no visible means of support. I think the grandmother gives him money from time to time out of what she has left," Kim said.

Lyon made a dollar sign in the column under Bates' name. He also wrote "stamp collector" and added the same notation under the Traxis column.

"Are you knocking out the Winthrops because they don't collect stamps?" Bea asked.

"We don't know if they collect stamps or not," Rocco said.

Lyon wrote "opportunity" in Bates' column and put a series of question marks after it. "Until we talk to Bates, we don't know if he has an alibi for the night Bea was taken prisoner."

"That knocks out Traxis," Rocco said. "We have proof he was at a town meeting during the time Bea was picked up."

"But his employee Reuven was home alone," Lyon added as he jotted the name in the Traxis column. He wrote "opportunity" under the remaining two columns. "Burt Winthrop had a motive in his desire to obtain Nutmeg Hill. The execution of the plan could have been carried out by his sons."

130

"And those twins have done just about everything else," Rocco interjected. "They have an arrest record in Middleburg that's an arm's length long."

"What in heaven's name for?" Bea asked.

"Hell-raising. Mostly drunk and disorderly, with one attempted rape. The rape charges were dropped when the woman involved refused to testify. They drink after work and get mean."

"What about Winthrop's finances?" Lyon asked.

"Shaky. As Kim found out, their development in Middleburg is in trouble. Their notes are overdue and their debt load is too high."

"He came up for the money for Nutmeg Hill fast enough," Lyon said as Bea winced.

"We suspect that came from something called the Xavier Corporation," Rocco said.

"And who's behind that?"

"We don't know."

Kim was on her feet. "All right, guys. I know, I know. Who owns the Xavier Corporation? I'm on my way."

"I'll go with you," Bea said. "I'm going stir-crazy sitting around the house."

"Make sure you take Jamie Martin," Rocco said.

"Come on. He follows us like we're trustees on a chain gang."

"He goes."

"Then can't he at least wear civilian clothes?"

"Have you ever seen Jamie in one of his suits?"

"No," Bea admitted, "I haven't."

"Believe me, keep him in uniform."

Lyon held a half-filled snifter of Dry Sack sherry in both hands as he sat before the blackboard and studied the diagrams and clues. The house was quiet. Rocco had had a drink with him and then gone home. Bea and Kim were still checking into the Xavier Corporation, and the ghosts of

131

their past life seemed to fill the rooms of this house they would soon have to leave.

He had added more items to the lists under the names on the blackboard. Most prominent was "Chloroform Charlie" under Traxis. He had placed four exclamation marks next to that entry.

A heavy pounding at the front door jolted him. His abrupt movement knocked over the chair. "Bea!" he said aloud. Something had happened to her. They had been ambushed, and Jamie Martin had been cut down before he could protect them. He dashed for the front door and threw it open.

The man on the front stoop burst into the hallway. His hands gripped Lyon's shirt front as his forward momentum crashed them against the wall.

"You bastard! You filthy bastard! Where is she?"

Lyon's shirt ripped as he forced the man's hands away. "Knock it off!" he yelled as his attacker hurled a roundhouse punch toward his head. Lyon threw himself to the side and the blow landed on the wall, causing his assailant to gasp in pain.

"Damn you!"

"Bates!" Lyon yelled. "Bates Stockton!" There was madness in the eyes of the man standing before Lyon. His face was contorted into a grimace of hatred.

"You couldn't leave well enough alone, could you? You had to ruin me in college and now you took my old lady. Why me, Wentworth?"

Lyon beckoned toward the study. "In here."

Bates glowered at him for a moment. He seemed to do battle with himself over taking another punch at Lyon or following his command; finally he stalked into the study.

Lyon followed his former student. Bates Stockton, after more than a decade, was little changed. His profusion of dark hair was beginning to be speckled with white, and the lines on his face were now etched deeper.

132

"A drink?"

"Something strong. Straight whiskey."

Lyon poured and handed the glass to Bates, who had slouched back in the leather chair. "You want to tell me what's going on?"

Bates drained his drink in two quick gulps and then fumbled in his pants pocket for a piece of paper, which he threw at Lyon's feet. "Read it."

Lyon stooped to pick up the note, smoothed it out on his knee, and read the few scrawled words. "I have gone away with the Wentworths. They are taking me to a place where you can't find me. I cannot be hurt anymore." It was unsigned, but it was obvious who had written it. "She's in a women's shelter," Lyon said.

"So I figured," Bates said as he dropped his empty glass to the floor. Two ice cubes slithered across the carpet. "I called a couple. The bastards won't even tell me if she's there or not."

"That's the way they operate."

"What put you on my case again?" Bate's eyes swiveled across the room and stopped at the blackboard. He took two steps toward the board. "What in hell is this?"

"Just some notes I made." He inwardly cursed himself for the lack of foresight that had let him bring one of the suspects into this room.

"What kind of notes?" Bates turned to face him with anger raging in his face.

"It has to do with my wife's kidnapping."

"You're going to try and lay that on me too. You never stop, do you?"

"She was held in the cemetery where your family plot is located."

"The Stockton Pie. Christ! That's a weed-choked anachronism. I haven't been up there since we planted the old man."

"You collect stamps."

"So do thousands of other. . . . Oh, the guy who pulled it off got paid in stamps."

"Something like that."

"And you came to my place to accuse me, right, teach?"

"To ask you certain questions."

"And you found the old lady whimpering in the corner."

"You had beaten her."

"You took her away in order to zing me."

"We took her because she had no other place to go."

"Bull! She had a place with me."

"She didn't want to stay."

"Listen, Wentworth. You screwed me to the wall once, but you don't get a second chance. Don't try and lay what happened to your wife on me. Understand?"

"You're only one suspect."

"No way! When did it happen?"

"The night of the twelfth."

"That leaves me out. That night I was tucked away in jail."

"Where?"

"A little town in New York State called Raleigh. So forget it. This is one you can't get me for." He stalked to the front door. "So lay off!"

12

LYON PULLED THE DATSUN between the parking lanes so that the car's nose pointed directly at the Murphysville Police Station. He turned off the ignition with a resigned flick of his wrist. He felt tired and knew that the feeling was caused by malaise and depression.

"Are any of the others here yet?" Bea asked.

Lyon glanced in both directions. The parking spaces before the station were vacant. "I guess not. Rocco wanted to talk to us first."

Murphysville's police headquarters was a new building in the sense that any construction within the past decade was considered new by the locals. It was a squat one-story building with oblong windows on each side of its glass front door. A massive skylight roofed almost half of the interior, and an abstract mural covered part of the right wall. Most townspeople said the art was a rendering of the Burning Bush; others argued that it was a nonrepresentational view of the hand of justice. Rocco insisted that it was the pointed index finger of the fickle finger of fate.

Lyon and Bea, followed by the ever-present Jamie Martin, walked up the short walk to the entrance. The heavy glass door opened into a four-by-six-foot anteroom facing a waist-high counter above which a thick glass partition rose to the ceiling. The harried communications clerk sat before a maze of radio equipment, ADT warning boards, and a computer terminal.

Jamie Martin tapped on the glass until the clerk turned toward him with a frown. He waved, and she pushed back a strand of long blond hair that had fallen over her forehead and smiled in return.

"Mr. and Mrs. Wentworth to see the chief," Jamie said through the intercom.

She held up a finger and turned to pick up the telephone. Cradling the phone on one shoulder, she entered their names on a sign-in sheet, then passed two plastic visitor's badges through a low slot at the base of the bulletproof glass. A door to the right of the communications module clicked open as she pressed the release button.

"Pin the badges on, please," Jamie said as he escorted them through the door and down the hall to Rocco's office.

Rocco was bent over a Mr. Coffee machine on the credenza behind his desk. He waved at them.

"What's with this new Fort Knox security?" Lyon asked.

Rocco shrugged. "It's the new first selectman's idea. He's afraid we'll be attacked by radical groups who will steal all our weapons."

"That was Dillinger's game, but he was killed forty years ago," Bea said.

"Maybe our new first selectman watches a lot of old movies," Lyon suggested.

"Could be," Rocco said as he served coffee without being asked. "All that I know is that it's a pain in the ass."

Bea picked up her Styrofoam cup with a broad gesture, took three steps to the window, and turned to face them. "I am going to finish my coffee. I am then going out to our car and driving to my office. No more of these endless meetings that don't seem to get us anywhere."

"They're all coming here this morning, Bea. It took

136

time and arm-twisting to set up, and I wish you, of all people, would be here."

"What's the agenda?" Lyon asked.

Rocco pulled a yellow legal pad from his center desk drawer and ticked off names with a slender silver pen. "They're staggered as to their time of arrival. We'll record everything, and Bea will watch through there." He gestured to a small mirror on the wall.

"One-way?" Lyon asked.

"Right," Rocco replied. "There's an entrance to a small room behind the mirror through the hall supply closet."

"I get claustrophobia," Bea said.

"You'll only be in there a short while," Rocco said.

"Thanks. And if I make a positive identification, I come through the looking glass."

"Something like that." Rocco reached into a side desk drawer and pulled out a tape cassette which he placed into a small player. He adjusted a small microphone on the edge of his desk. The intercom buzzed and he picked up the phone.

"Mr. Traxis is here to see you," they heard the woman at the front desk say.

"Send him in."

Lyon wondered if things weren't more rational when the Murphysville police headquarters shared quarters with the tax assessor's office and the town library. In those days security had consisted of placing the room key over the door molding. Visitors were shunted by an aged lady who acted as secretary, radio and telephone operator, and librarian. The inexorable march of progress was turning their small town into a gigantic corporate headquarters.

"I'd better go to my compartment," Bea said as she hastily rushed for the door. She turned with her hand on the knob. "By the way. Traxis is one of the principals in the

Xavier Corporation. In other words, he and the Winthrops are in bed together." She left the room.

"Well, I'll be damned," Rocco said.

Robert Trainor Traxis wore a conservative pinstripe business suit that Lyon estimated had cost several hundred pounds in London. The lines of the suit hid the bulk of his pyknic physique and gave him a taller appearance. His bald head glistened, but his facial features were now nearly expressionless.

Traxis sat stiffly on the straight chair in front of Rocco's desk. Lyon lounged on the couch to the side.

"As a good citizen, I am honoring your request, Herbert, but this is the last time. You are disrupting my schedule. In addition, I am sure that Wentworth has informed you that I was at a town meeting on the night Mrs. Wentworth was kidnapped."

"I have a copy of the minutes for that meeting," Rocco said. "You were certainly there during the time period in question."

"Then our business is concluded." Traxis half rose in his chair until Rocco extended a hand and gestured for him to remain seated.

Traxis sank back reluctantly. From across the room, Lyon could see a small muscle in his cheek begin to throb. The man was angering.

Rocco opened a folder. "There are a couple of items that I would like to go over."

Traxis spoke abruptly. "I think I've had just about enough." He held up his right hand and began to tick points off in an angry staccato. "Item: I collect stamps. Rebuttal: So do a million other people, thousands in the state of Connecticut alone. Item: I make frequent trips to England. Rebuttal: I have a legitimate business reason to so do. Item: I have a dislike for Beatrice Wentworth. Rebuttal: I stand not alone. She is one of the most controversial figures in the state senate. Need I say more?"

138

"How much do you dislike Bea Wentworth?" Rocco asked mildly.

There are code words that tend to trigger explosions in persons of narrowly focused convictions. Lyon watched with a certain morbid fascination as Traxis burst out, "She stands against everything sacred to our nation. Her sanctimonious backing of welfare cheats and other boondoggle programs is a rape of the middle class for the benefit of the shirkers. Her stands on feminism are a feeble excuse for the emasculation of all men."

Bea, sitting on a high stool in the cramped room behind the supply closet, looked out through the mirror into Rocco's office. She was staring into the face of Robert Traxis and realizing that she was seeing a man ravaged with hate. Hate directed toward her. She felt a cramping in her stomach and shivered in revulsion.

"Do I want her annihilated?" Traxis continued. "You bet your bottom dollar I do. I want her politically dead and expunged from any position she holds in our government."

"Shipped back to where she belongs?" Rocco suggested.

"She was born in Rocky Hill, Connecticut," Lyon said. "That's about a five-minute row across the Connecticut River."

"If you were half a man, Wentworth, you'd stand up to your wife and keep her home where she belongs. Or did she crop your balls long ago?"

Lyon catapulted from the sofa and took two steps toward Traxis before Rocco reached him and held him back.

"I know what all of this amounts to," Traxis said. "This whole damn meeting has nothing to do with some so-called kidnapping. It's dirty politics. You want me to shut up about her. This meeting is a thin disguise to muzzle me. Well, it won't be done. I will not leave her alone."

"Get out of here," Rocco said quietly but with an ominous edge to his voice.

"Damn right!" Traxis stormed from the room.

Lyon shook off Rocco's arm. "I don't know what that little incident proved. We already knew how he felt."

"You knew. I had only heard secondhand." Rocco made several notes in the folder.

"His alibi is tight."

"And he has enough money to hire any damn hood he wants."

"For God's sake, Rocco. Upper-middle-class industrialists don't exactly move in the same social circles as hired guns. How many cases do you know where housewives have tried to recruit killers in bars to do their husbands in?"

"And half the time they seem to approach off-duty cops." Rocco laughed. "What about the hood Traxis already has working for him?"

"Is Reuven coming today?"

"A little down the list. Our next guest is your friendly neighborhood builder."

Burt Winthrop knocked his boots together before he sat down and flaked cakes of mud across Rocco's floor. He smiled affably and waved at Lyon on the sofa. He gestured over his shoulder toward one of his sons who stood in the doorway. "Sit down, boy."

Rocco frowned. "Which one is he?"

"That's Roy," Winthrop said as the twin sat on the edge of the sofa as far from Lyon as possible.

"Where's the other one?"

"We're not rich kids like the rest of you," Burt said. "Someone has to mind the store. We've got nailing and selling to do. Talk to one of the boys, and you've talked to them both."

"The law does not exactly consider people carbon copies of each other, Burt," Rocco said.

140

"Come on, Chief. Get on with it," the builder said impatiently. "We've got foundations to enclose."

"You or your boys collect stamps?" Rocco asked offhandedly.

"Stamps? We probably got some postage and documentary stamps for deeds in the petty-cash box."

"Postage stamps," Rocco pressed.

"We use a meter," Roy said eagerly from his heretofore silent spot on the couch. "You put the letter in one end of this little machine and turn the little handle, and it comes out sealed and stamped."

Rocco sighed. "Even we have one of those. That wasn't exactly what I meant. Let's try another area. You're involved with the Xavier Corporation."

"We got a lot of different corporations. Hell, each one of our jobs is a different one. It's smart business. If the job goes sour, we can fold our tents and it don't hurt anything else we got on the drawing board."

"And cuts off the legs of your subcontractors," Lyon said in a low voice.

Burt Winthrop glared at Lyon. "What's that got to do with you, Wentworth? They're big boys and know the rules of the game. Besides, you just can't walk away from a job anymore. The banks have gotten sensitive and don't want to foreclose. They'll haunt you forever and dry up your credit. It ain't like the good old days when you could play games."

"The Xavier Corporation," Rocco said again.

"It's a financial company we set up to obtain venture capital."

"And Robert Traxis is an investor?"

"We have several money backers."

"And you used the money from that company to buy Nutmeg Hill?" Lyon asked as more of a statement.

Burt Winthrop shrugged. "So?" He looked slowly from

Lyon to Rocco. "What gives? What does any of this have to do with Bea Wentworth getting snatched?"

Rocco turned to face Roy. "Tell me about the night of June the twelfth."

The twin looked blank. "That was a couple of weeks ago."

"Make a stab at it."

"Gee, I don't know. I'd have to look at a calendar and count back."

There was something about this splinter off the professional country boy that bothered Lyon, that gave him a feeling, without a logical basis, that there was more here than was being displayed.

Rocco pointed to a calendar on the wall. "Are the numbers and letters big enough?"

"Sure. I think that was the night my brother and I banged a couple of college chicks in Middleburg."

"Are you sure?"

"I think so. I can confirm it with my brother."

Burt Winthrop smiled benignly at his son's recitation.

Lyon repeated the phrasing "my brother and I" to himself. He had it. The speech patterns of the professional country boy the younger did not match the words and delivery of Winthrop Senior. "Where did you go to college, Roy?"

Roy smiled at Lyon with an ingenuous grin. "Wesleyan."

"Political science or history?"

"Both. A major in history and a minor in poli-sci."

Burt Winthrop winced. "You trying to destroy our image, Wentworth?"

"Does it really help sales?" Lyon asked.

"Who knows? But when you negotiate, every small edge helps. Better people think Roy and I got walking-around IQs than any of that fancy college stuff."

"Quit the games," Rocco snapped. "I want to know the names of the girls you partied with that night."

"Mine was a girl called Gretchen Fowler. Rob's girl was Lucy Something-or-other."

"How about finding out who Lucy Something is and calling me?" Rocco said.

"Is that necessary?" Roy asked.

"You can bet your country-boy manner it is," Rocco snapped as he shoved a legal pad at Roy. "Now write down Gretchen's address."

Lyon hardly recognized Bates Stockton. His hair had been cut and styled, and he wore knife-creased gray flannel slacks, a navy-blue sport coat with gold buttons, and a regimental tie. His Gucci loafers were shined, and he shook hands with Rocco with a sincere, junior-executive combination of self-confidence and deference to authority. Bates sat down on the side chair and waved at Lyon. "Hi there, Mr. Wentworth."

Rocco was puzzled. He glanced through Bates' folder again as if he had been missing something. "Thank you for coming, Mr. Stockton," he finally said.

"If I can be of any help, sir."

"I understand that you know the Wentworths?"

"Mr. Wentworth only. I have never had the pleasure of meeting his wife."

"In what capacity did you know Lyon—Mr. Wentworth?"

"Years ago he was my faculty adviser."

"And you had an altercation?"

"I wouldn't exactly call it that."

"Over a matter of plagiarism."

"It wasn't quite that serious, Chief Herbert. There were some similarities between my thesis and a previously published work, and rather than redo the work, I opted to leave school."

"Without hard feelings?"

Bates shrugged. "Disappointments fade in time. I'm not a baby, Chief. The problems of life that seemed important years ago are not quite as painful today."

"Where were you the night of June the twelfth?"

Bates laughed. "That happens to be a night I remember well, as it is the only time in my life that I was incarcerated."

"Explain that."

"I was driving back to Connecticut from a job interview in Syracuse, New York. I stopped in a gin mill in a little town near the state line. I guess I had a snootful and passed out on the shoulder of the road. The local gendarmes put me up for the night—in a cell."

"What town?"

Bates hesitated a moment. "Same name as a southern city. Ah . . . Raleigh. Yes, Raleigh, New York."

Rocco glanced quickly over to the couch. Lyon knew by the glance that Rocco had already verified Bates' alibi. The interview with the former graduate student was only a formality to satisfy the Wentworths.

"Thank you for coming by, Mr. Stockton," Rocco said.

Bates walked toward the door and gave them a short farewell wave.

"You didn't see him at the house when he attacked me," Lyon said.

Rocco picked up a folder. "Obviously he was on his best behavior, but I've called Raleigh, New York. Bates was in their lockup that night." The intercom buzzed, and Rocco picked up the phone and grunted an acknowledgment. "Reuven's on his way in."

Bea burst into the room and threw herself on the couch next to Lyon. She looked slightly disheveled and blotted her face with a paper towel. "That cubbyhole is a miniature Black Hole of Calcutta. It must be 120 degrees in there."

"Any of them resemble the guy who took you?" Rocco asked.

Bea shook her head. "You can rule out Traxis and Burt; their ages aren't right. But the twins and Bates . . . it could be any of them."

"Then pay particular attention to our next visitor. Reuven is the right age, has a prior record of similar attacks, and works for Traxis."

"You think Traxis paid him?"

"I think he's capable of it. You had better get back to your peephole."

"Let me face this one straight on," she replied. "It's death in there, and recently I don't care for confined places."

"If you insist." Rocco bent over the tape recorder, jotted the time on a pad, and turned the cartridge over.

"It would seem that everyone involved has an alibi except Reuven," Lyon said.

Rocco's pencil tapped impatiently on the desk. "I want Bea to see Reuven. We'll talk a few minutes, and then I want to sweat him—alone."

"I just want this over with," Bea said tiredly.

"Where the hell is he?" Rocco snatched the phone receiver from its cradle and punched in the communication clerk's number. "Where's the last guy who came through?" he barked. He listened a moment. "It takes ten seconds to walk down the hall. Send Martin in here."

In seconds there was a soft knock on the door as Patrolman Jamie Martin stuck his head in the room. "You wanted me, Chief?"

"A guy just checked in the station and never showed in my office. Look in the john. Go through the whole damn building in case he's wandered off."

"Right." The door closed.

Time hovered over the room. Each was lost in thought. Rocco, the most impatient, tapped his pencil. Bea, the most frightened, braced herself for the coming interview.

The door burst open and startled them from their reveries.

Jamie Martin, his face ashen, leaned into the room with both hands clutching the door frame. "I found him."

"Well, damn it! Let's get this show on the road. Get him in here."

"It's not that easy, Chief."

"Is he some sort of reluctant dragon or something?"

"Not exactly. He's dead."

13

THE BASEMENT FLOOR of the Murphysville police services building contained a pistol range, three holding cells, a small gymnasium, and a boiler area. The three holding cells were directly across the hall from the firing range. Two of the cells were empty. Reuven was hanging in the third.

Bea took one look, turned away, and entered the open door of the first cell, where she sat on the bunk and put her head between her knees.

Lyon and Rocco stood in the cell doorway with Jamie Martin hovering behind them.

"Well, I'll be goddamned," Rocco whispered.

"Let's get him down," Lyon said as he rushed to the rear of the cell, where Reuven was hanging suspended by a belt from the small grillwork that covered the high, narrow window. Lyon yanked at the belt unsuccessfully until Rocco came to his aid and lifted the body high enough to allow for slack. Lyon ripped the belt from the dead man's neck, and Rocco let the corpse topple over onto the bunk.

Lyon knelt next to Reuven's head and pried open his mouth in preparation for mouth-to-mouth resuscitation. He looked up at Rocco. "Do you know CPR?"

"We're all certified in it, but it's a waste of time. He's gone."

"It can't be. There wasn't enough time."

"I've seen too many." He turned to Jamie Martin. "Call the medical examiner."

"Yes, sir." The patrolman bolted for the stairs.

"Wait a sec," Rocco called after him. "You had also better call Captain Norbert at the state police barracks. We'll have to have an outside investigation of this one." He shook his head sadly. "In my own police station yet. Good God, why? You know what Norbie will think. You know what the newspapers will make of this."

"That you were sweating him and he took his own life."

"You're damn right! That's the story that will be spread over the whole damn state." Rocco rushed down the hall to the wall phone by the stairwell. He flipped the receiver into his hand and clicked impatiently for the communications clerk. "This is Herbert. Don't let anyone except official personnel enter or leave this building. That's a firm order." He slammed the phone down and walked pensively back to the cell. "What in hell are you doing?"

Lyon had emptied Reuven's pockets and spread their contents over the blanket next to the body. There were the usual pocket items such as wallet, comb, handkerchief, and key ring. He held a single loose key in his hand and displayed it to Rocco. "Any ideas what this opens?"

Rocco took the key. "It looks like a padlock key."

"Want to make any bets?"

"No."

"Who has the lock that held the mausoleum door shut?"

"Norbie has all that material."

"You had better ask him to bring it along when he comes over here."

Rocco stomped back to the phone. "Why did he choose my police station to hang himself? He could have used a tree. There's a fine tree on the town green where several people have been hanged."

As Lyon bent over the body, he decided that strangulation was a hard way to die. The belt had dug deeply into the neck, leaving a broad swatch of discolored flesh. Reuven's eyes protruded slightly, and their sightless stare contained a mass of broken blood vessels that radiated out from the corneas.

Lyon surveyed the cell. A three-legged stool lay turned over on its side by the door. "He could have stood on that while he attached the belt," he said.

"Uh-huh," Rocco agreed. "And then kicked it away."

"In a scaffold hanging, the springing trap drops the body and breaks the neck, causing immediate death," Lyon said. "Reuven died of strangulation."

"He probably knew we were zeroing in on him and couldn't face doing more time."

"You're convinced he killed himself?"

"Aren't you?"

"I'm not certain." Lyon squatted by the cell wall underneath the window grille. He ran his fingers lightly across the surface. "You keep a clean jail."

"Hell, nobody's hardly ever here except for a few drunken housewives."

"You wash the cells down regularly?"

"A cleaning woman comes in once a week and does them top to bottom. You won't find a roach anywhere."

"Nor a scuff mark."

"What's that mean?" Rocco asked with a puzzled frown.

"I don't care how much a man wants to die, when that belt tightened around his neck, there had to be automatic struggling."

"Sure, and he'd reach up and try and pull up on the belt."

"His feet would flail. His heels would have kicked against the wall."

Rocco knelt and ran his hands over the clean surface. "And there aren't any marks."

"Exactly." Lyon returned to the bunk and bent over the body. He gingerly spread the neck flesh apart.

"Don't fool with the merchandise until the ME gets here."

"Look at this." Rocco bent over the corpse. "See the deep narrow gash under the belt bruises?"

"Oh Jesus," Rocco said. "That's a wire-ligature mark."

"Right. Reuven was garroted with a thin wire until he was unconscious, and then he was hanged by the belt from the window grating.

"The son of a bitch was murdered."

The official chroniclers of the violently killed began to gather in the narrow hallway in the basement of the police services building. A doctor knelt on the cell floor next to the bunk and examined the body while a police photographer stood in the doorway shooting pictures from different angles. Two paramedics lounged against the wall near the phone smoking while their gurney with its empty body bag waited nearby.

Captain Norbert and two accompanying corporals stalked down the hall. He glanced contemptuously into the cell containing the body and then turned angrily to Rocco. "Don't you take a man's belt before you lock him up?"

"Usually."

"You sweated him, right? And then you threw him in here to think things over." He waved a deprecating arm across the small cell. "Not even closed-circuit TV monitors. You small-town cops are all alike. What'd you do, Herbert? Stick his dick in a light socket?"

"That's enough, Norbie. I did not beat the slob. I never even saw him come through the front door."

"Hear no evil, see no evil. And I bet every damn cop in town will back you up. Boy, talk about cover-ups."

150

Bea came out of the cell where she had been sitting. "Will you two stop it! Don't you have an investigation to run or something?"

"Something like that," Rocco replied. "You bring the lock, Norbie?"

"Lock. Lock." Captain Norbert snapped his fingers, and one of the corporals produced an evidence bag containing the broken lock. Rocco took it gingerly, opened the bag, and inserted the key Lyon had found into the keyhole. He slowly turned the key.

"It fits."

"Looks like we've got the kidnapper," Norbert said. "Too bad he's dead."

"You two are too much." Bea started down the hall. "I'll be in Rocco's office if anyone needs me."

The medical examiner turned away from the body. "Mr. Wentworth is right. This man didn't hang himself. He was strangled from behind, probably with a piece of piano wire."

"Even we small-town cops aren't that merciless," Rocco said.

The paramedics moved forward with their gurney and prepared to take the body away. Norbert gestured to the second corporal, who produced a small hand vacuum which he proceeded to move slowly across the floor of the cell.

"All right, Herbert. Tell me what's going on."

Lyon stepped around the senior police officers and opened the door to the small gym. Barbells and exercise machines cluttered the room. It was empty of people, and there were no closets, windows, or exterior doors. He continued down the hallway to the boiler room. It, too, was empty. The narrow firing range was not in use, although a vague smell of cordite permeated the firing lanes.

The only entrance to the basement was the lone stairwell at the far end of the building. The only windows were

151

those high on the holding-cell walls, and they were covered with a heavy metal grating.

He mounted the stairs to the main floor and opened the first door off the hall. The room contained fingerprint equipment and a camera mounted on a tripod. Rocco's office was next, and then came the youth-services room, occupied by a single desk and two chairs.

On the far side of the hall was an open area with half a dozen school desks interspersed throughout its space. It also contained a bank of vending machines, a large bulletin board, and a water fountain. This was the assembly room for the small shifts that Rocco mounted to protect the citizens of Murphysville.

Lyon walked slowly through the building, opening office and closet doors. It was midshift, and except for the murmur of the men downstairs, the main floor was quiet. The communications officer sat by the front door eating a tuna fish sandwich. A single uniformed officer was typing with two fingers at a desk behind the radio equipment. There was no one else on the floor.

It was a well-lit building, relying for its cheerful interior on natural sunlight falling through a dozen vertical windows and a large skylight. Lyon stood behind the communications module and stared up at the skylight, which was V-shaped with the glass slanting to a central support beam. It was double-thickness safety glass, strong enough to support a heavy snowfall and without openings or breaks. The other windows were constructed not to open due to the central heating and air-conditioning.

A whooping alarm went off!

Lyon's body jerked at the alien sound. He turned toward the communications desk and saw that the clerk looked as puzzled as he felt. The only other exit from the station was the heavy metal door that led to the rear parking lot.

The two paramedics with their shrouded body on the

gurney stood half-in and half-out of the rear entrance looking perplexed.

"Who the hell did that?" Rocco bellowed from downstairs as he took the steps three at a time.

"We didn't know, Chief," one of the paramedics replied.

"I told you the front door," Rocco shouted over the sound of the alarm.

"The ambulance is in the rear and we just thought . . ."

"Never mind." Rocco stretched toward a metal box mounted directly under the alarm at the right of the rear door. He pressed a red reset button, and the alarm immediately stopped.

"Sorry about that," the second paramedic said as they rolled the gurney back into the building.

"You're out now," Rocco said. "Go on." He waited until the gurney was out of the door before he pulled it shut and reached for the control box and pressed the reset button again.

Lyon had walked down the hall toward the angry Rocco. "That's the only other exit out of here, except through the front, isn't it?"

"Yes. This door is locked and can only be opened from the inside by pressing down on the bar. Either way, it sets off the alarm."

"Then the murderer did not go out this back door?"

"Not hardly," Rocco said.

Lyon walked back the length of the building to the communications desk. He glanced at the name badge on the woman's uniform shirt. "Elsie Summers," it read. She looked vaguely familiar, like a caricature of someone he had once known.

"Can I see the sign-in sheet?" he asked.

She squinted up at him as irritation briefly flicked across her features, to be replaced by a broad smile. "You're Lyon Wentworth."

153

Lyon took the clipboard containing the list. "Yes."

"When I was in high school you spoke to our English class. I even read one of your books, *The Wobblies Take Over.*"

"I hope you liked it," Lyon said as he glanced down at the list. Their names were all there, with the times they had arrived. Only his and Bea's names were still open, without a sign-out time.

"Is it true that the Wobblies are symbolic of the hidden forces of good and evil?"

"I suppose so." He handed the clipboard back. "The officers on duty don't sign in?"

"Chief Herbert felt that would be carrying things a little too far. I mean, there aren't that many and I know them all. Besides, they have to punch a time clock when they come on and off a shift."

"But no one else comes in or out without going past you?"

She nodded in agreement. "No one."

"But if you have to leave your post for a minute or two . . ."

"One of the other officers sits in while I'm gone."

"Did anyone this morning?"

"No. I haven't left since I came on duty at eight."

Lyon tapped the clipboard. "Are you absolutely positive that no one else except those on this list came in here this morning?"

"I'd swear to it."

"Thank you." Lyon walked pensively down the hall toward Rocco's office. Unless one considered the preposterous idea that one of Rocco's people had committed the murder, everyone else was accounted for.

Everyone but Bea and himself was signed out—but that was impossible.

He turned and hurried back to the desk. "Let me see that list again."

She handed it to him without a word.

Reuven had been signed out.

A dead man had been officially logged out of the building.

"Something wrong?"

He turned the board around so that she could see it and ran his finger along Reuven's line. "According to your records, this man left the building."

She looked up at him with astonishment. "That's the dead man."

"Yes."

"He couldn't have signed out."

"You don't happen to remember the person who went out?"

She shook her head. "I'm sorry. I could have been on the phone or busy doing something else and just didn't pay attention."

"You had better take good care of that sheet; it's going to be needed." Lyon started back to Rocco's office.

In the chief's office, Rocco and Bea were huddled over the desk. Rocco was working with the tape recorder, and Bea held a stopwatch in one hand, a pencil in the other.

"Now," Rocco snapped.

Bea clicked the stopwatch, looked at the time, and wrote it down. "Got it."

"What are you two doing?" Lyon asked.

"We recorded everything that happened this morning," Rocco said. "That will give us an exact fix on the time everyone entered and left the office."

"That'll help. I checked; there's no way in or out of this building except through the front door, and no one is hiding in here."

"I could have told you that."

"Reuven is signed out," Lyon said.

"What?"

"Somehow Reuven was signed out in that new system you have at the front door."

"That doesn't make any sense," Bea said.

"Maybe it does," Rocco said as he took his place in the desk chair and tilted it as far back as it would go. "I can hardly tell the Winthrop twins apart. Suppose Roy, or whoever it was, came in with Burt, then the other one presents himself at the receptionist's window and says he had to get something from the car. She lets him in."

Bea nodded. "That puts two of them inside, but only one is signed in. The second twin leaves and signs out in Reuven's name . . . after killing him."

Rocco tilted his chair forward with a crunch. "Makes sense." He looked at Lyon expectantly. "It solves our problem. We had a guy loose in here in perfect position to slip a wire around Reuven's neck and carry him downstairs to the cell."

Captain Norbert did not open doors, he flung them against walls. Rocco winced as the door handle dug into the plaster. "You can have your station back, Herbert. We've got everything we need from down there."

"You come up with anything?"

"Take a couple of days for the lab people to go through it. We're going to pick up Traxis for interrogation. He's our man, no doubt about it."

"Traxis?" Lyon and Bea said in unison.

"Hell yes!" the state police officer bellowed. "He paid Reuven to snatch Bea; the key proves that. He was afraid Reuven would break under questioning, so he eliminates him."

"Can you prove that?" Rocco asked.

"Now that we have the scenario, we can fit the pieces together." A smirk cleaved his face. "These crumbs always make mistakes. We get them in the end." He waggled a finger at Rocco. "Better keep a sharp eye on your shop, chief. Can't have this sort of thing happening right under our noses."

The door slammed and Norbert was gone. They could hear his progress down the hall and waited expectantly for the slam of the front door. It came, and Bea smiled at Lyon.

"Jesus H. Christ!" Rocco said. "After this, the first selectman is going to make me plant a mine field in the flower bed by the front door."

They were silent a moment before Bea spoke. "It seems obvious that Reuven's death and my kidnapping are intertwined. Rocco thinks it's the twins working for their father with avarice as the motive."

"Best motive there is."

"Norbert thinks it's Traxis," Bea continued. "Motive ideological."

"Maybe more than that," Rocco said. "There is that financial link between Winthrop and Traxis."

She turned to Lyon. "And then there's your ex-student."

"Motive, revenge," Lyon added.

"I've been a cop a lot of years," Rocco said. "And in my experience, I don't know of a single case where someone harbored a grudge for fifteen years before acting. Feelings tend to dissipate if they aren't acted on at once."

"Whoever did it still has the stamps," Lyon added. "You can increase everyone's motive by the financial worth of those stamps."

14

ELSIE SUMMERS STOOD IN the center of Rocco's office and
smoothed down her skirt. She was obviously trying to look
efficient and businesslike.

"It is possible, isn't it, Elsie?" Rocco asked.

"No, sir. I'm sure it isn't."

"You remember Mr. Winthrop Senior?"

"Vaguely, sir. I mean, I didn't notice him in any particular way."

"Then how are you so sure that Rob-Roy, whoever the
hell it was, didn't pass in twice?"

"I think I would have noticed him."

"They are identical twins that even their own goddamn
mother can't tell apart."

"I just would have noticed."

Rocco's temper erupted as his fist thudded onto the
desk with a resounding crack that made the young police
officer jump. "You wouldn't!"

Her hand brushed her cheek, and Rocco became visibly
embarrassed at his browbeating. "I just would," she insisted.

"You noticed Roy Winthrop in particular?" Rocco asked
nearly in a whisper.

"Yes, sir."

"What made you single him out?"

A slow flush began to seep up from the collar of her uniform shirt. "He . . . he stopped by my desk a second and spoke to me."

"What did he say?"

"I'd rather not repeat it, Chief." She gave a furtive glance around the room, as if looking for an avenue of escape.

Rocco forced himself to be calm. "Elsie, you handled the rape interro last year. We've trained you to repeat nasty things."

"Well, this was addressed to me personally."

Bea took the police officer gently by the sleeve and led her from the room. She glanced in Rocco's direction, and the large chief nodded his acquiescence.

"I've got a murder in my basement and an upstairs full of people who all seem to be out to lunch."

Bea returned with a red face and whispered in Lyon's ear.

"Well, I'll be damned," Lyon said.

"For God's sake, what is it?" Rocco nearly yelled.

"Forget it," Lyon retorted. "It's not germane to the case but just proves that she really would remember Roy."

"What is this, a conspiracy?"

Lyon bent over the desk and hastily wrote on the yellow legal pad, ripped the page off, and handed it to Rocco. "For your file. Elsie's direct quotation."

"About time." Rocco grabbed the sheet and scanned the words Lyon had written. His fists balled into massive clumps. "He can't talk that way to one of my people!" He rushed around the desk and headed for the door as Lyon intercepted him. "I'll cream the bastard!"

"No way," Lyon said as he pushed his friend back around the desk and into his chair. "I don't care what Roy said; Norbie would have you up on assault charges."

"It would make his day," Rocco agreed.

"Look in your notes," Lyon said, "and tell me exactly what you have on Bates Stockton's alibi."

Rocco grunted and began to leaf through his bulky file. He located a letter written on cheap letterhead and looked up at Lyon and Bea. "I asked for a written confirmation. Bates claims that on the night of the kidnapping he was incarcerated in a local jail in Raleigh, New York. That's a little town just across the border on the Hudson River. I called the chief over there. He confirmed the alibi, and here's what he wrote me." Rocco began to read the awkward sentences. "'A report was received on the afternoon of June 12 at 1530 hours that a body was located on the shoulder of Route 52. A car was dispatched and the subject was picked up by Officer James R. Easley, shield number 3. . . .'"

Bea giggled. "Shield 3?"

For the first time Rocco smiled as he looked over the top of the letter. "Evidently Raleigh is even smaller than Murphysville."

"On with it."

"You ought to see the typos in this letter," Rocco said. "Anyway: 'The subject was obviously under the influence of intoxicating liquor or controlled substances.' That's dope," Rocco added.

Lyon sighed. "Uh-huh."

"Anyway," He began to read again: "'subject was brought to headquarters. Documentation on subject's person, in the form of a social security card, library card, and letters, identified same as Bates Stockton of Connecticut. Subject was held overnight and released on the following morning at 0900.'"

"So much for that," Lyon said.

"We've still got to check the twins' alibi for that night," Bea said.

"We will," Rocco said. "You know what gets me?" He waved an arm. "When we built this place, we put in a foolproof security system. No one, but no one, gets in this building except through the front door, where they are checked in. We know the alarm system was operating and working because it went off accidentally when the paramedics tried to go out through the back door."

"As best I can determine," Lyon said, "at the time of the murder, Jamie Martin was in the station house with one other officer and the clerk at the front desk."

"I've known those people since I was in grade school," Rocco said. "Well, not Jamie and Elsie—I've known them since *they* were in grade school and I used to do school crossings. I'd stake my life on any of them."

"Why don't we finish working with the recorder," Bea said. "It will give us a time fix that we can compare to the sign-out sheet. It might tell us something."

Bea and Rocco huddled over the small machine as Lyon walked back into the main part of the building. Little had changed, and it was oppressively quiet. At the front desk, Elsie Summer was still busy. Her movements, as she turned from radio to front desk and around to the telephone, reminded him of the little tramp's activity as he worked on the assembly line in the movie *Modern Times*. There was a relentless, nearly frantic movement to her body, and it was no wonder that she was vague over identification of anyone except Roy.

"Elsie, are all the badges accounted for?"

"Yes, Mr. Wentworth."

He walked pensively back to the office. Rocco looked up as he entered and switched off the recorder. "We've got it; like a look?"

"Sure would." Lyon took the pad with Bea's meticulous notes and slouched down on the couch to read the time breakdown.

Rocco had made a notation of the date and time when the first visitor, Traxis, had been announced. The tape had continued running until they had all left the room at the announcement of the discovery of the body. Names and times were specific:

Name	To office	Left Office	Signed Out
Traxis	9:21	9:45	9:46
Winthrops	10:01	10:15	10:17
Bates	10:31	10:50	10:53
Reuven	11:07 (in bldg)	Never arrived	11:19

"Whoever killed Reuven had twelve minutes to do it in," Lyon said.

Rocco looked depressed. "It would seem so."

"And during that time no one else came in or out of the building."

"It's a slow day," Rocco said. "If I didn't have a murder in my basement, I would hardly know what to do with myself."

Bea took the notes off Lyon's lap. "There must be a clue in here somewhere." She ran her finger down the names and times. "How do we know that someone puts down the right time?"

"There's a clock right next to the sheet by the door," Rocco said. "Whoever's working the desk enters the time. There could be a slight error of perhaps a minute or two, but no more."

Bea shook her head. "I don't see it then. There's probably something here staring us in the face, but I don't know what it is. Someone had to kill Reuven, return his badge, and leave the building in his place. How could that be? Everyone else signed out. There was no one in the station except us and three officers on duty."

"Holy Jesus, Bea," Rocco said, "if I knew the answer to that, I'd have myself a murderer. I can't even figure out how it was done without worrying about how they got in here."

"I think I have something on that," Lyon said. "Let's re-

162

create it." He walked into the hallway, followed by Bea and Rocco. "Whoever it was, whether one of the people we interviewed or someone else who gained access to the station, they stood in this room." He walked into the room beyond Rocco's office, which contained the fingerprint equipment and camera. "This room is hardly ever used and was almost certain to be vacant during the time we're interested in."

"Sometimes we book and print a perp every other week," Rocco said.

Lyon stood in the corner of the room beyond the door. His position gave him a clear view of the hall nearly to the front desk. "I can see anyone coming down the hall."

Rocco and Bea hovered near him and checked the sight lines. "Reuven would be coming toward my office next door," Rocco said.

"The killer stepped out into the hallway when he saw him coming. Reuven had never been in this building before, had he?"

"Not to my knowledge."

"He or she stepped into the hallway and beckoned to Reuven. The victim responded, and they went down the steps into the basement." Lyon turned the corner and started down the stairs toward the holding cells. "He let the victim proceed ahead by three steps. When he reached the basement level, the killer slipped the wire over Reuven's neck. He probably placed his knee in the small of his back and twisted the wire."

"And no one heard a sound," Bea said.

"If the garrote is closed firmly and quickly enough, there's no possibility of the victim making any sound except perhaps a low gurgling that wouldn't have carried to the top of the stairs."

Rocco nodded. "Then he dragged the unconscious body into the open cell, took off the victim's belt, and hanged him from the grillework."

"And then dropped the key in Reuven's pocket, took

the victim's badge, and signed himself out in the murdered man's name," Bea said.

"That's all just dandy," Rocco said. "Except how in hell did he get in here in the first place?"

Captain Norbert's amplified phone voice filled Rocco's office. As usual, Rocco sat with his chair pushed back and his feet on the desk. Lyon and Bea sat together on the couch.

"I'm drawing up the search warrant now," Norbert said. "Since Reuven had a room in the Traxis home, we have every right to toss the whole damn place."

"You had better make the warrant as inclusive as possible," Rocco said. "Anything you find not on the list is tainted evidence."

"I know that! Why in the hell do you think I'm calling you? I'm going to tell the judge that Reuven was a prime suspect in a kidnapping, attempted murder, and conspiracy. In addition, since he was a murder victim, we need a thorough search. Which is all going to give us one hell of a good shot at Traxis."

"What do you have on the warrant so far?"

"Ski masks, chloroform, the list of valuable stamps, and any evidence of van keys. We're still looking for that sucker."

"None of the suspects has a van registered to him?" Bea asked.

"Hell, no. We checked that out a long time ago, but they could have rented one under an assumed name or stolen one. Can you think of anything else to include?"

Rocco looked at Bea and Lyon as they shook their heads. "That's it, Norbie. Good hunting."

"Would that we were so lucky." The connection was broken, and the hum of the dial tone filled the room.

"What would we have to find in order to indict Traxis?" Lyon asked.

Rocco's feet clumped to the floor as he leaned across

the desk. "Well, a diary, written in his own hand with a signature at the bottom of each page wherein he confessed to everything in sufficient detail for us to find other corroborating evidence, would help."

"I'm serious."

"In the first place, I don't bring the indictment, right? Norbie prepares the information and evidence and sends it to the state's attorney, who would issue a warrant . . . maybe. Then we go before the grand jury, who may or may not make a presentment; then we go to trial."

"You're a big help."

"Sorry. My cynicism increases with the years. It's getting harder and harder to get these guys, Lyon. If he walks in here with the loaded gun still smoking and confesses in the presence of his lawyer . . . then we have a good case."

"If not?"

"Then Norbie has to find something awfully incriminating. With Reuven dead, it's going to take very hard evidence to bring charges against Traxis."

"You're attacking my liberal sensibilities," Bea said.

"When I was in London and told the fellows over there our rules on evidence, Miranda and the whole smear, they were rolling in the pub aisles."

"I'm surprised to hear that," Lyon said. "The English judicial system has always seemed very fair to me."

"It is," Rocco said. "They have a sense of fair play over there that is not to be believed, and that's what's saved them. They aren't hobbled like we are because they never abused the system in the first place."

They stood in front of the police station blinking in the warm afternoon sun. Lyon felt tired. The kaleidoscope of events had been disconcerting.

"I had better go grocery shopping," Bea said in a quiet voice.

165

"I'll drive you to the shopping center and browse in the bookstore."

"I don't think I'm up to the shopping center yet. I'll just pick up a few things at Walt's Market."

He glanced at her with concern. "You feel all right?"

"Are we caught in some web that's going to entangle us the rest of our lives?"

"He'll be caught, or he might already be dead."

"Maybe." Bea, followed by Jamie Martin, started across the street and up the short walk to the green and Walt's Market. Lyon knew she did not care to shop there. It was expensive and catered to older women who ordered single chicken breasts and had the order delivered.

"I'll meet you back at the car," he called after her. She didn't answer and continued up the street. Her shoulders were slightly hunched forward, and her steps were hesitant, as if the forward motion of her body had to test the firmness of the way before she shifted weight to the next step.

His wife had been violated. The shock of the trauma was still festering. It was this limbo in which they were existing that continued her fear.

He had read that women who had been raped were never again the same. Forever after they shied from dark corners and never felt a true sense of security.

This was why men often yearned for the combat of war. The necessity to face a known enemy of physical proportions could be a relief from nameless fear.

There was something about his earlier recapitulation of the murder that bothered him, and he thought he knew where to find the answer.

Lyon turned and began to walk back a block to the Murphysville Town Hall.

There was a small bag of groceries in the rear of the station wagon when Lyon returned to the car. Bea was sitting in

166

the front seat on the passenger's side looking straight ahead. She gave a start and glanced at him apprehensively when he opened the door.

"Where's Jamie?" he asked.

"Gone."

"Gone where?"

"I don't want any more guards or keepers. One way or the other, I've got to get through this without Jamie and his shotgun."

15

"I AM NOT GOING to eat breakfast sitting on the kitchen floor."

"Lean back against the cupboards. It's really quite comfortable," Lyon said as he demonstrated.

"This is nonsense."

"You always said the kitchen floor was clean enough to eat off."

"I didn't mean that literally." Bea grasped the edge of a kitchen counter and pulled herself erect. She began to do busywork around the coffee percolator.

"You're in the line of fire," Lyon said softly. "Anyone with a high-powered rifle could get you through the window." He pushed her shoulders gently until she took two steps away from the window.

"I'm not going to live this way, Lyon. I want to go back to work. I want to go to the Capitol and do my business, and go shopping again. I want to live normally."

"I suppose we could eat in the cellar."

"We are going to eat in the breakfast nook in exactly five minutes. I will then go to work and you will take your bod into the study and attempt to write great children's literature."

He knew her mind was set, and he slid into the nook.

They were midway through fat western omelets when

the car careening up the drive caused them both to stop eating with forks poised in midair. "You know that's Rocco," Lyon said. "In five seconds he'll be in here demanding coffee."

"Where's the coffee?" Rocco said from the kitchen doorway a few moments later. "There's good news this morning."

"We could use some."

Rocco pulled a mug from a cabinet and filled it with coffee. "Norbie and the boys tossed the Traxis house last night. . . ."

"And?"

Rocco slid into the breakfast nook and whipped a Polaroid snapshot from his pocket. "It's almost the smoking gun," he said as he handed the picture to Lyon.

Lyon examined the picture a moment. "It's a United States 1918 24-cent inverted airmail."

"You're damn right it is."

"That's one of the ransom stamps," Bea said.

"Found in the Traxis private collection. Didn't he tell you that he didn't have an inverted airmail?"

"Yes, he sure did."

Bea smiled. "Traxis knew that Reuven had been asked to headquarters for an interrogation."

"We call them interviews now," Rocco corrected.

"He was afraid that I might identify Reuven, which would implicate him."

"That's how we see it," Rocco said.

"You know there were a hundred of those inverted airmails on the original sheet," Lyon said. "Traxis could have bought one honestly."

"And lied to you."

"True."

"Traxis has one; he lied about it."

"He has the money to buy it legitimately."

Rocco shook his head. "Reuven snatched Bea, held her,

and Traxis collected the stamps in London. Reuven had the MO for what he did, and Traxis had a double motive."

"What about the other stamps?"

"They haven't turned up yet, and we assume that he sold them in Europe."

"Is it enough for the grand jury?" Bea asked.

"Norbie's with the state's attorney right now. It's going to be a tough one, what with the rules of evidence being what they are and the high-powered legal talent we can expect Traxis to muster. But we'll get the bastard—if we have to plea-bargain with him."

"Plea-bargain!" Bea spluttered. "How can you say that? I spent days locked up in a hole. I died half a dozen times. I don't want any plea-bargain."

Rocco looked beseechingly at Lyon. "Bea, we may have to. The evidence is circumstantial, and with Reuven dead, there's no living witness."

"I'm the evidence," Bea said firmly.

Rocco hesitated. "Well, to tell you the truth, we've let Traxis know that you are prepared to identify Reuven as your abductor."

"Oh, great!" Lyon said as he slammed down his cup. "And where is he now? You know, he may be out to kill Bea."

"We've thought of that," Rocco said softly. "Which is why he is under constant surveillance."

"And if he makes an overt move against Bea, you've really got him."

"Something like that."

"I'm not sure I like being the fox in this game," Bea said.

"I wouldn't do it if I wasn't completely satisfied as to your safety. Traxis will always be under watch."

"What about Reuven's murder?" Lyon asked. "Are you going to try and nail Traxis on that?"

"Hell! We can't even come up with how it was done."

"Have you gotten the address of the girls the Winthrop twins were with the night Bea was taken?"

Rocco looked at him quizzically. "Yeah. But I haven't had time to track it down and don't see that it makes any difference now."

"I'd like to."

"Be my guest. Call me at the station, and I'll give you the address." He placed a hand on Bea's shoulder. "I promise it's going to be all right, and we're going to nail him."

Bea gave him a limp smile.

Lyon glanced down at the slip of paper on the car seat by his side and then up at the street sign. He turned the car down Warren Street and peered at front stoops for a legible house number. The street, filled with two- and three-family frame dwellings built along a tree-shaded sidewalk, was located two streets away from the campus of Middleburg College.

Number 322 was on the right-hand side of the street, and he was able to park directly in front of the walk. A G. Fowler was listed on the mailbox located on the porch. He pressed the buzzer under the box.

No answer. He rang again. Still no answer. The box indicated that G. Fowler lived in apartment 2, which he imagined was the upper unit. He tried the door and found it opened directly into a narrow hall with steep steps leading to the next floor.

"Anyone home?" he called.

Again no answer. He started up the steps. The door at the top of the stairs was partially ajar, and he pushed it open. "Anybody here?" he called again.

The dull whir of an ancient refrigerator was the only sound in the small apartment. He stepped inside.

The rooms were furnished in early trash. A short hallway, narrowed by several large green plastic bags stuffed with unimaginable objects, led into the living room that ran the length of the building. Overstuffed chairs in conflicting color schemes were piled high with newspapers and old magazines. A table by the front window had the remnants of several meals cluttering its surface.

"Anyone home?"

"Yeah," a voice answered. "Out here."

Lyon followed the sound of the voice and went through the living room into the kitchen to the double windows at the far end of the room. A small porch, its balustrade covered with hanging sheets, functioned as a sun deck. The blond girl on the large beach towel was nude. He half turned. "Oh, pardon me."

"Hey, wow, you've come to attack me, huh?"

"I don't think so."

"You're uptight around people with no clothes on."

"You could say that."

She climbed in the window, brushing up against him in the process. She ran the cold spigot at the kitchen sink and splashed water on her face. "It's hot out there."

"They say too much sun isn't good for people of light complexion," Lyon said.

She shrugged naked shoulders. "All the fun things aren't good for you. What can I do you for?"

"Do you always greet callers without any clothes?"

"Usually." Her hips canted to the side in a caricature of sexuality.

"I want to ask you about some people we both know."

"Sure. Shoot." She turned from him and ran half a glass of water into a misty jelly glass. She palmed a yellow pill into one hand and gulped it down.

She was a young woman still containing partial traces of plump adolescent sexuality, and yet her body was thin. Lyon realized that he was looking at someone who had recently lost a great deal of weight and had still not conceptualized the loss into her own sense of identity. An offshoot of the speed addict. "You know Rob and Roy Winthrop?"

"Sure." She went into the living room, threw a pile of newspapers on the floor, and plunked down into a fading red armchair. "The terrible twins. They're a thousand laughs."

"Were they here the night of June the twelfth?"

She shrugged again. "If they say they were here, they probably were. We party a lot."

"You and a girl called Lucy?"

"Lucy's always ready for a good time. She crashes here most of the time. She's probably in class now."

"You both go to Middleburg?"

Again the shoulder movement. "I don't go anymore, but my folks think I do." Her eyes narrowed, and she straightened her frail body. "Hey, now! My dad hire you to check up on me? Are you a private investigator or something?"

"No."

"Then what's with the questions?"

"It's important to me that I know where the twins were that night."

"They were probably here."

"You'd testify . . . swear to that?"

"Listen, mister, I don't even know what day of the week it is. If they say they were here that night, they were here. Like I said, we party a lot."

"Then you don't really know?"

"I don't really not know." She walked toward him with an exaggerated sway of her hips until she stood directly in front of him. "You want to make it with me?"

"Why do you ask that?"

"'Cuz I been out there in the sun thinking sexy thoughts, and it made me horny. Besides, I never made it with a guy your age."

Lyon was shocked to realize that her blunt statement had caused a reaction within him and he had nearly reached for her, if only to prove that youth had no monopoly on sexuality. He felt only slightly older than she. His internal clock had stopped somewhere in his twenties, and unless he looked in the mirror intently or exercised little-used muscles, he still felt on the cusp of thirty. She obviously did not view him that way, and he was chagrined to realize that he wanted to change that perception in this wandering girl-child. "Not today," he finally replied.

Her smile was skewered. "You don't ball girls, or you're over the hill, huh?"

"Neither."

"You'd better go, mister. I don't like old guys staring at my bod and thinking dirty thoughts." Her petulance camouflaged his rejection.

Lyon started for the door. "Is there any way you can reconstruct what happened the night of the twelfth?"

She held to the door frame and swayed slightly. "Who the hell knows? The days and nights are all the same, aren't they?"

"Maybe so." He started down the stairs and could feel her presence behind him. Her eyes had compressed into a squint that would in the near future change to astigmatism. He felt the ripples that she radiated of a hopeless future.

"And don't come back!" she yelled after him as she slammed the door.

He thought about lost young people as he drove back to Murphysville. During the years he had taught, he had seen the few that began to nod in class. In the beginning they forced themselves into occasional attention, but gradually they gave up and attended class only spasmodically and showed little interest, until they stopped attending at all. They sometimes lived in dorms, but more often in off-campus housing, and the drugs-and-liquor combination

174

changed from weekend parties to a way of life that spiraled them into stupor and lethargy.

He forced the girl from his mind. The twins would reach her soon, if they hadn't already. She would be their alibi, and undoubtedly there would be others who would swear to their presence during the party in the trash-strewn apartment.

Bea was right.

They were living on the battlements of fear, a fear so all-encompassing that it was dictating their movements. It would continue. Traxis would be charged—maybe—and he would walk free on bond pending his trial a year or two hence. And they would continue to live in fear.

It had to end.

He knew what had to be done and the critical risk that Bea would have to take.

He drove the last few miles thinking about the two phone calls he would have to make: one to verify a suspicion, the other to ensure a course of action. The second call would have to be worded strongly, very strongly.

16

LYON STOOD OUTSIDE THE Murphysville police station with a stopwatch clutched in his right-hand pocket. As he walked up the short walk to the front door he set the watch in motion.

He stepped through the door into the small anteroom before the communications desk. Elsie Summers looked up and waved at him through the glass.

"Rocco wants me to look at a file on his desk."

"Sure thing, Mr. Wentworth." She made a note on the sign-in sheet and slid a visitor's badge through the small aperture in the glass. Lyon stuck the badge into his pocket so that the edge was exposed. Elsie glanced at the clock by her side, noted the time on the clipboard, and pressed the buzzer releasing the door.

With a wave, Lyon stepped inside the station. "Thanks." He walked briskly down the hall toward Rocco's office. It was twelve-fifteen, and he knew that Rocco would be at Sarge's Place for at least another half hour. There would be plenty of time to do what had to be done.

He continued down the hall past Rocco's office and stopped near the rear door and the stairwell that led to the basement. He turned to look back down the corridor. There was no one in the hall, and little other movement or sound inside the nearly deserted station house.

Lyon stretched toward the alarm system hung high on the wall near the stairs. He flipped the "off" switch and watched the red indicator light flick off. He went back down the hall to Rocco's office and let himself inside.

The cabinet containing the articles he needed was against the far wall, secured by a heavy padlock attached to wooden paneling.

He pulled up his pants leg and ripped off the screwdriver taped to his ankle, wincing at the sharp pain caused by the adhesive's removal. He inserted the screwdriver into the holes at the end of the hasp.

The screws had been countersunk and were difficult to turn. He strained on the screwdriver until the first one began to turn in its slot.

It took him four minutes to remove the remainder of the screws and fold the hasp away from the paneling. The doors to the cabinet could now be opened.

From time to time Rocco had displayed the police department's newest equipment as if they were newly discovered toys that would never be used. Lyon knew where to find the items he needed, and he quickly took them off their shelves.

He took down one of the bulletproof vests that had recently been purchased by the town.

"For our SWAT team," Rocco had said with a laugh. "As soon as we form one."

Next he selected a starlight scope and carefully laid it on the floor next to the body armor. The scope was an electronic device that amplified dim light and helped surveillance teams penetrate the darkness.

"Great for getting the goods on flashers," Rocco had said.

The final item was a pump-action .12 gauge shotgun with a short barrel. He checked to see that the magazine was full. There were weapons at the house that Rocco had

177

forced on him, but to prove his point he felt it necessary to take another.

He removed the plastic lawn bag he had tucked around his waist and placed the stolen items inside.

He closed the closet doors and debated over reinserting the screws. He decided not to and left his tools neatly aligned on Rocco's desk. It would give his friend pause when he discovered them.

The lawn bag was too bulky to carry past the communications desk without comment, but he had never intended to do so.

Carrying the bag, Lyon peeked out of the office to find the corridor still empty. He stepped into the hallway, shut the door behind him, and walked the few feet to the rear door, which he carefully opened. He placed the lawn bag outside against the side of the building.

He closed the rear door, checked to make sure it was secure, and reached up the wall to switch on the alarm. The red indicator light flashed on.

At the communications desk he flipped the visitor's badge to Elsie, saw her log the time, and left the building. As he walked down the walk toward the driveway leading to the rear of the building he clicked the stopwatch and took it from his pocket. Seven minutes had elapsed.

Lyon stood on the widow's walk of Nutmeg Hill, trying to decide from which direction the attack would come. The trap lines had been strung, and Bea was the bait. It was now imperative that he calculate the direction that the killer would take.

It would be tonight. The phone calls had set the events in motion, and the killer would feel trapped by the time limitations Lyon had created.

Lyon turned toward the river. From his position at the apex of the promontory, the river below seemed distant. Attack from that quadrant would be very difficult. The killer would have to float down the river in a small, silent craft and anchor it below the house. It would then be necessary to climb a nearly sheer cliff, and even if successful, he would end up below the terrace with a poor field of fire.

At this point the Connecticut River was nearly a half mile across. The rocky shoreline at the far bank was even more formidable than on this side. A firing position in the trees across the river would require an accurate shot of nearly 880 yards. It was not an impossible shot by an expert marksman, assuming his weapon was properly aligned and zeroed and he took proper compensation for the brisk river winds, which shifted constantly; but it was an improbable one, with many chances of error.

Lyon turned around. From this vantage point he could see the secondary highway at the end of their long curving drive. He knew from experience that at this time of year only the chimney of the house was visible from the road. It seemed doubtful that the attacker would park so conspicuously.

On the left side of the house, beyond Bea's garden, were nearly impenetrable rows of bramble bushes. He had attempted to trim the area last fall, and the countless scratches and cuts he had suffered attested to the difficulty anyone would have in trying to crawl through that maze of underbrush.

The attack would come from the right. The lawn sloped gently toward a stand of pine that stood on a low ridge. When darkness fell, tree shadows would provide excellent cover, and the ridge height would give a rifleman the distinct advantage of unobstructed sight lines to the house.

"Lyon." The trapdoor at the end of the widow's walk raised as Bea stuck her head over the edge. "Rocco's on the phone. He's pretty upset and wants to send Jamie Martin over here."

"What did you tell him?"

"Nothing, but he insists on talking to you."

"Be right there."

The concern in Rocco's voice was obvious. "Traxis is gone."

"What does 'gone' mean?"

"It means he slipped away from the guy watching him. Damn fool!"

"Was it an obvious attempt, or did the guy on surveilance just slip up?"

"We're not exactly sure, and we hope to pick him up again soon. It was the oldest gambit in the world. He drove to a drugstore and went in. Our guy sat in his car for fifteen minutes before he became suspicious and went into the store. There was a back entrance that Traxis must have used."

"Then he went off without his car?"

"The car was gone when our guy came back out. Listen, this worries me. You know that Traxis thinks Bea can ID Reuven, which brings the whole mess right to his doorstep. If you don't want Jamie out there, I'll come myself."

"No, Rocco."

"What do you mean, no?"

"No bodyguards."

"I'll stop in for a friendly drink and stay until they pick up his trail again."

"You'll stay all night and leave your car in the drive. No."

"Are you up to something?"

"After all that we've been through, we want to be alone. Can't you understand a simple thing like that?" Lyon inwardly cringed at the tone of his voice.

There was a pause on the other end of the line. "It's your life, old buddy." Rocco was miffed. "I've got better things to do tonight. Somebody tinkered with my supply closet."

"Call you in the morning," Lyon said and abruptly hung up.

180

"You weren't very nice," Bea said.

"We can't have him out here tonight." He looked over at Bea, who was standing by the kitchen counter in a floor-length granny dress. "That is singularly unattractive."

"I thought you'd like it."

"It looks like Mother Hubbard's nightgown. How does the vest fit?"

Bea thumped her chest and produced a soft clunking sound. "It's huge on me and comes down below my bottom."

"That one was made specifically for Rocco. You could probably fit three of you in there. Did you cut out part of the back like I asked?"

"Over there." She pointed to the counter, where a pile of the rear portion of the jacket lay.

Lyon hefted the cut remnants in his hand and looked out the window. The day was dying, and once the final rim of sun sank below the hills, dusk would quickly deepen. "We don't have much time." He took a portion of the cut vest and placed it around her neck.

"That's going to be pretty obvious, isn't it?"

"Not when we're through disguising it."

Fifteen minutes later Bea Wentworth sat in deep shadows in a chair on the patio. The vest remnants were around her neck, covered by a large towel she had wrapped around her shoulders and neck. Most of her head was encased in an old-fashioned hair dryer that was supported by a metal stanchion. The floodlamps attached to the house gutters would cast a bright swatch of light across the patio when they were turned on.

"Where in the world did you get this dryer?"

"It was stuck back in an attic corner."

"No one uses these things anymore. Everybody has a blow dryer."

"I'm counting on the fact that our killer won't know

that. I had to have protection for your head." Lyon stepped back through the French door. Bea was as safe as he could possibly make her. From the protection on her neck to the rim of the hair dryer, only a few inches of her face were visible. He counted on the fact that the sharpshooter would notice this and decide on an easy body shot.

"A question, Went. If you're going to grab the guy before he shoots . . . why all this protection?"

"Added precaution. You okay?"

"Nervous as hell. You had better get on your way, it's almost dark."

Lyon left the house through a darkened cellar window. He slid behind a row of bushes that masked the side of the house. He wore a dark poplin jacket with a rain hood that fastened tightly over his head. A flashlight was in his back pocket, the starlight scope was strapped to him, and he cradled the shotgun in his arms. He slithered down the bush line toward the end of the house.

There was a slight dip in the yard at the corner, and if he moved carefully in the darkness, he would not cast a silhouette that would be visible from the pines on the low ridge to his front.

It took him ten minutes to work his way across the broad expanse of lawn to the tree line. He lay quietly for a few moments at the base of the ridge and listened. The night was filled with sound, crickets chirped, and the faint scratch of nocturnal animals could be heard. Everything seemed natural. He gave a short lunge and rolled under the shadows of a low pine tree.

He turned to face the house. He could see the light in the kitchen, and the reflected light from the lamp in his study. Bea was still shrouded in darkness on the patio. In minutes she would throw the switch and be illuminated by the patio floods. He was very near the position that the gunman would probably assume.

Lyon squatted near the base of the tree and again listened to the night sounds. He could not detect any alien movement and began to work his way down the inner line of trees toward the far end of the promontory.

He knew the place he had selected well. It was a rock cropping perched on the edge of the cliff high above the slowly moving Connecticut River. He wedged himself between two boulders that would give him flank protection. His field of vision extended down along the pines that marked the edge of the woods and also along the lawn leading to the house.

The patio lights flicked on and instantly revealed Bea. She held a book in her hands, but as time progressed, he saw that she did not turn the pages.

He unstrapped the starlight scope and arranged the flashlight and shotgun by his side. He adjusted the scope and began to examine the line of trees to his front.

The attack would have to come from that direction. There was no other position that allowed a clear shot of Bea on the patio.

She would stay on the patio for ninety minutes and then hurry into the house. Whatever was going to happen must occur within that time span; if not, they would have to try again tomorrow night.

With the passage of time, Lyon's eyes adjusted to the dark, and with the aid of the starlight scope he had a clear view of the ridge line.

It was an interminable wait. His hands gripped the pistol grip of the shotgun with perspiring palms. He worried that if he raised the barrel it would wobble, but assured himself that it wouldn't matter how accurate his aim was. All that he had to do was point in the general direction of his adversary.

He hoped it wouldn't come to that. He hoped that his

superior position behind the marksman and the bright glare of the flashlight would force an immediate surrender.

A half-moon scudded behind fast-drifting clouds and the tree line to his front darkened into deep shadows. The night sounds seemed to fade until all that he could hear was the rustle of a light breeze through the tops of the pines.

The press of metal against the nape of his neck was unmistakable.

He hadn't heard a sound.

Someone crouched behind him with a knee pressed into the small of his back. One hand pushed his face deep into the leafy-dirt surface while the other held the pistol firmly against his head.

"How dumb do you think I am, Wentworth?" The voice was low, nearly guttural. "I learned. I learned to survive in the jungle. And you sent me there."

"I had nothing to . . ."

The barrel of the pistol slammed against his cheekbone, and pain radiated down his jaw. He gave an involuntary grunt.

"You sure in hell did. When you turned down that thesis I spent a year of hell over there. And after that it was downhill. Each year, as things got worse, I thought of you and how you caused it. Now, it's pay-up time."

"You lived through it, Bates. That's important. We can . . ." Again the side of the barrel smashed into his face.

"Not another word. What's with you? Did you think I was going to stroll up here and take a shot at her from some obvious spot?" Bates bent toward Lyon's ear and spoke in a whisper. "We're going to move up to the tree line. We're going to the exact spot where you thought I would go. If you do not do exactly as I say, I will kill you first. Now, get slowly to your feet and move ahead of me to the trees. Now!"

Lyon felt the muzzle pressed firmly against his back as

he moved forward. Bea was clearly outlined in light on the patio. As they approached the tree line of pines, she stood and placed her book in the chair seat. The ninety minutes were up. In seconds she would be out of the frame of light and safely in the house.

"Damn!" Bates shoved Lyon forward with such force that he tripped over a root and fell. He rolled over to see that ten feet away Bates had dropped the pistol and pulled off a rifle slung on his back. He cradled it in his arms with the sling wound around his arm as he snapped it to his shoulder and took a quick sighting.

Lyon rolled over to his hands and knees. "Bea!" he screamed simultaneously with the rifle shot.

The high-powered projectile hit Bea Wentworth with several thousand foot-pounds, flinging her across the patio and over the edge of the parapet.

Lyon instinctively somersaulted while the afterimage of Bea's shooting seared him. On his feet, he ran toward Bates Stockton as the rifle swiveled in his direction.

Lyon dived and caught Bates with his right shoulder as they both fell.

Bates struggled to his knees and held the rifle by the barrel and swung it at Lyon. It missed by inches.

Shots.

Evenly spaced shots with a crescendo that reverberated over the hills.

Bates dived for the protection of a tree trunk, the fallen rifle forgotten for the moment.

Bullets cracked overhead. Lyon realized that they were being fired from somewhere near the corner of the house and were hitting the trees and piercing the foliage several feet above their heads. Whoever was shooting was aiming high.

Lyon scuttled back through the trees toward the edge of the promontory and his equipment. He frantically searched through the dried leaves between the rocks for the shotgun. His fingers passed over the stock, and he pulled the weapon toward him.

The firing had stopped.

The heavy boom of the weapon that had aimed over their heads had to be a .357 magnum, the weapon that Rocco carried.

Lyon turned toward the tree line with the shotgun at his waist.

Bates seemed to rise out of the darkness before him. He had retrieved his handgun and held it in his right hand while his left supported his wrist. It was aimed directly at Lyon's chest.

Lyon had only to move the shotgun a few inches until it pointed directly at Bates.

"It's a standoff, Wentworth, but with a difference. I can do it and you can't. I'm going to waste you."

The night was clear and nearly bright as clouds moved away from the half-face of the moon. They stood on the edge of the rock face high over the water, and Lyon could clearly see Bates' features. He knew the man was going to shoot him. The pointed weapon was only a few feet from his sternum. The bullet would rip into his chest, and he wouldn't even hear the sound of its retort.

"You know, Wentworth, you never did have any guts. If you did, you would have blown me apart with that bird gun you're holding. You had your chance. Now I'm going to give it to you in the face." The handgun moved inexorably up Lyon's body toward his head.

A montage of pictures flipped past Lyon's eyes with blurring rapidity: the gaunt hollow look on Bea's face when he had released her from her confinement, the ill look on her face as she looked at the hanged Reuven, and the final and ultimate picture of her thrown off the parapet with Bates' well-aimed shot.

His finger tightend on the shotgun trigger.

Bates' grimace was a malevolent grin in the shaft of moonlight.

Bates' skewered smile turned to astonishment as he jerked forward against Lyon's body. They both sprawled in the dead leaves as the loud retort of the magnum echoed among the rocks.

Lyon turned his head to see the bulky shadow move cautiously through the woods toward them.

17

"I CRUSHED A BED of chrysanthemums," Bea said with a wry smile. "Help me get this thing off." Her hands shook as she tried to sip brandy from a small snifter.

"I thought you were dead," Lyon said as he peeled the granny dress off her shoulders and pulled it down. She obediently turned and he began to undo the flak vest.

"For a moment I thought I was. That thing hit me like a sledgehammer, and I lost my wind when I landed on my back in the garden."

His fumbling fingers finally removed the last of the restraints, and he tenderly lifted the heavy vest off her body and let it fall to the floor. There was an ugly red welt in the center of her chest just above her bra. "My God!"

Bea looked down at the bruise with a bemused smile. "He was a good shot, wasn't he?" She sank heavily down into the leather chair in Lyon's study and gripped the snifter with both hands. "Let's not spend any more evenings like this for a while, okay?"

"We won't have to," Lyon replied as he poured a pony of sherry and straddled a chair in front of her. "He's dead."

"Rocco did it?"

"Yes. Both he and Bates saw through my rather transparent ploy. Rocco parked at the foot of the drive and pulled the cruiser in the woods. He was walking up to the house when Bates fired at you."

"Thank God."

"Yes." Lyon walked through the study into the living room. He could see the ridge line out the window. Men with powerful flashlights were moving in the woods like ghoulish fireflies as they gathered the debris of death. Photos would be taken, shell casings would be picked up with tweezers and placed in evidence bags, and then Bates' body would be removed in a rubber bag and it would be over. Lyon had almost failed. The risks had proved unacceptable, and only the fortuitous arrival of Rocco had saved them from annihilation. He returned to his wife.

They sat quietly to wait for Rocco, Lyon's thoughts on that instant when he nearly pulled the trigger. He had given the burden of death to his friend to carry.

It was twenty minutes before they heard the slam of the kitchen door and Rocco's footfalls through the house.

The police chief looked tired and haggard as he came into the study and mixed a strong vodka and orange juice at the bar cart. He took a hefty swig of his drink and glowered across the room at Lyon. "You know, old buddy, you cut it awfully close. If I had taken another two minutes to make up my mind about coming out here, you'd be the one in the body bag."

"I'm glad you made it," Lyon said.

"And you!" Rocco pointed a finger at Bea. "How dumb can a smart lady like you get? Letting yourself be used as bait like that was nothing but stupid."

"Lyon had it worked out."

"So tell me."

"My plan called for me to get him before he got into firing position," Lyon said. "The body armor was backup."

"And where was the backup to the backup?"

Lyon nodded. "I didn't foresee that he would be that

189

good in the woods. I made the major error of underestimating him."

"Did you know it was Bates, or did you just throw it out and see who you'd net?"

"I knew it was Bates. I called him earlier."

Rocco took another sip of his drink. "I had my money on Traxis. I was surprised as hell to see who it was I had shot."

"It had to be Bates," Lyon said. He nodded toward the wall where the unerased chalkboard still stood. It seemed an eon ago that they had all sat in this room compiling clues and motives for him to list on the board. "Outside of ourselves and Norbie's people, Bates Stockton was the only other person who was aware of who the other suspects were. He was in this room and had ample time to see the columns on the board and Reuven's name in the Traxis column."

"Makes sense. A good clue, but nothing we could use for a warrant. So, based on that guess, you made a call to set Bates up. What in the hell did you say to him that got him out here tonight?"

"I reverted to the outraged teacher," Lyon said. "I started out coldly, pedantically, and told him what an idiot he was. I informed him that we had a voice identification from the tape we made of the kidnapping call. He told me that was impossible with the laryngophone. No one else except the authorities knew about the method of voice disguise, and that's when I knew I had him."

"He could have run."

"I went on to tell him that Bea was prepared to identify him. We were both going to see the state's attorney first thing in the morning, and if he came around Nutmeg Hill tonight, I'd blow his head off with my .45."

"So he knew you were in the house, alert, armed with a handgun."

"I thought that would preclude him from rushing the house and force him to take a shot from the woods."

"By the way, I found our starlight scope and shotgun in the woods, and I would imagine that mangled vest on the floor is mine. You sure in hell didn't walk out of the station house carrying all that junk. Want to tell me how you did it?"

"Nearly the same way as Bates did when he killed Reuven. Bates signed in, talked to us, and when he left your office he threw the alarm switch and propped open the rear door with something like a match cover. He was then able to sign out and let himself in the rear door. He killed Reuven and signed out in that name."

"Too pat," Rocco said. "You saw me turn off the alarm system; I don't see how a stranger would know how it worked."

"The plans and specifications for the whole building, including the wiring schematics, are on file at the town hall. They are open to anyone's inspection."

"Oh Christ, we spend thousands on a security system and then advertise it. The records are with the minutes of the town finance committee, right?"

"That's where I found them."

"Wait a minute," Bea said. "Bates Stockton was in a small town jail the night I was taken."

"That's right," Rocco agreed. "You saw the file on that, Lyon. I made a call and we have a follow-up letter from the chief in Raleigh."

"I heard you read a letter that said a Bates Stockton was picked up, identified by such things as a social security card and personal mail, and held overnight. It was my guess that he wasn't officially booked."

"The letter didn't mention it, and small towns don't usually book on a drunk charge; might prove too embar-

191

rassing if they brought in a local resident. So, no booking, no fingerprinting and FBI identity verification."

"Someone else used Bates' name."

"A hired stand-in."

"Right. Bates let him out in Raleigh and picked him up the next morning. It's my guess that somewhere between here and Raleigh, New York, we're going to find the body of a nameless derelict."

"I'll check that one out."

"With a good alibi like that, why did he bother to kill Reuven?" Bea asked.

"He knew that his alibi would not stand close examination, and when he realized that we were only working with three groups of suspects, he had to relieve the pressure on himself. Reuven's death and the padlock key we found should have removed him from the list completely."

Bea yawned. "Now, if we only had the stamps back, we might sell them and buy back our house."

Lyon looked pensive. "Could you do something for me, Rocco? I don't think Bates had time to sell the stamps yet. I think he still has them."

"That's not much to go on. The man is dead, and those stamps could be anywhere. I doubt that we'll ever find them."

"People, even men as bright at Bates, act in patterns. Whatever happened to him, Bates always returned to his grandmother's house in Fernwick. She still keeps his room and all of his childhood things. Try there. Look in that room, particularly in his very earliest stamp albums."

"Would somebody do something for me?" Bea asked.

"What?"

"Please get me a robe. I'm cold as hell."

Lyon sat on the edge of the patio parapet with a mug of coffee in his hand. Bea was directly below him in the garden, doing her best to resurrect the crushed flowers. He didn't have the heart to remind her that it really didn't matter. In two weeks they would have to leave Nutmeg Hill, and the condition of her flowers would matter little to earth-moving machinery.

It was a fresh day with a slight breeze off the river and a clarity of sky that seemed to enhance all colors. He glanced up the ridge line toward the stand of pines that had nearly been fatal to them the night before. The trees swayed gently, and any ghosts that might inhabit the glen were dormant.

This was their home. Once they both had had every expectation of spending the remainder of their lives here. He glanced down at Bea. Her vitality and her old elan had returned . . . that was what mattered. They could find another place to live.

Rocco's police cruiser rocked up the drive and skidded to a halt by the front door. It was followed by Burt Winthrop's battered pickup truck. Rocco slammed from the cruiser and waved as he started around the house to the patio. Men jumped down from the back of the pickup and began to unload equipment from its bed. A heavyset man in khaki work clothes and high boots pitched a transit over his shoulder and began to walk to the far edge of the property.

The surveyors were here, the point squad of the demolition that would follow.

"Good news," Rocco said when he reached the edge of the patio.

"I could use some," Lyon said as the surveyor unfolded the tripod legs of his transit and began to adjust the instrument.

"We found the stamps. Damned if they weren't stuck away in a kid's stamp album. Can you beat that? A half million in stamps intermingled with others that were probably ordered from the back of a comic book."

"Were they all there?"

"Every damned one. And we got a bonus. Your prints and Bates' were both lifted from several of them. Great physical evidence. I also talked with the grandmother. As we suspected, she's been supporting Bates all these years, but it had come to an end. She gave him two thousand last month, but that was to be the last of it. She said he flew into a rage when she told him and screamed that it would all have been different if he had his degree, and you were to blame. So much for my theory of ancient revenge."

"I was his rationalization."

"Real to him."

"I was the symbol." Lyon looked out over the hills. "Well, now you can close the case."

"You know it." Rocco leaned over the wall and waved to Bea. "Hi."

She waved back and continued with her work.

"While they were lifting the prints I called our philatelist friend in New York," Rocco continued. "He's willing to buy back the stamps at the same price."

Lyon looked surprised. "Not wholesale?"

"Nope. It seems that for some perverse reason that only stamp collectors fathom, the damn things have actually increased in value."

"When could we get the money?"

"Right away, I guess. If he'll let me hold the stamps in escrow for a short while, I don't see why he couldn't pay you tomorrow."

There was hope. Lyon looked toward the far corner of the lawn where Burt Winthrop, standing with one of his sons, was examining the old survey map showing the perimeters of Nutmeg Hill. "Burt!" Lyon called. "Burt Winthrop, can I talk to you a minute?"

"Want to see you, too," Winthrop called back as he walked toward the house. "I was wondering if you and the little lady can get out of here earlier? I could sure use another week or two to get my models up before fall." He walked onto the patio and turned to face the house with arms akimbo. "These old places are a bitch to take down. Walls are too damn thick, with lots of supporting timber. If I can get the permits, I might blow it."

"What?" Bea poked her head over the parapet. "Blow what?"

"The house. A few pounds of the old TNT placed in the right places and—boom!—we got toothpicks."

Lyon and Bea cringed. "That's what I want to talk to you about, Burt. I want to buy the place back."

"Buy it back!" There was astonishment on the builder's face. "Are you pulling my leg?"

"No. I'll give you your money back with interest for the time I've had it."

"Interest? I'm talking millions here, Wentworth. This little old place is going to crawl with condos."

Bea started to climb over the wall. "Now wait just a minute!"

Lyon helped her over the wall and blocked her from a frontal assault on the builder. The potential fracas was diffused when a small, dusty VW scuttled up the drive. The car stopped behind the pickup, and a state trooper immediately got out from behind the wheel, hurried around the small car, and opened the passenger door with a flourish. A slight woman, barely five feet tall, left the car and waved at them.

"It's the governor," Bea said as she hurried across the patio.

"Beatrice, the state police commissioner called and told me what happened out here last night. How dreadful," the governor said. Both women threw their arms around each other.

Lyon watched the VW as the trooper pushed the front seat forward and Kim Ward unlimbered from the compact vehicle. She hurried toward Lyon as Bea and the governor huddled together in intimate conversation in a corner of the patio.

"You did it, old wise one," Kim said as she embraced Lyon. "Kooky, but you did it, and that's all that counts. If it helps any, I finally traced the van he used. It belonged to his grandmother. Like most other things in his life, she bought it for him."

"Can I go back to the surveyors now?" Burt Winthrop asked.

"We're not through with you," Rocco insisted as he shoved the builder back into a wicker chair. "You know, Burt, you're going to be watched real careful on this job. I mean, the building inspectors of this town are going to crawl all over you."

"You don't scare me, Herbert. I've had that problem before. A year from now I'll be off this job and counting my money."

"With a pocketful of profit."

"You know it. It's a dream situation. This is the best site in the state as soon as I get that monstrosity of a house off here."

The governor turned toward them. "What house?"

Bea put a restraining arm on the governor's shoulder. "It's nothing, Ruth. Just a little personal difficulty."

Winthrop looked up at the widow's walk. "Maybe we'll just let the dozers push it off the cliff. The whole smear—boom!—right off the edge."

"Nutmeg Hill!" the governor said in an incredulous voice.

Kim spoke in an aside. "The Wentworths had to sell the house to raise the money for the ransom."

"And this bastard won't sell it back to them," Rocco said.

"That's a disgrace." The governor glared at Winthrop.

"The house goes, lady," retorted Webster.

"It's governor, not lady," Rocco said.

"If I had wanted a governess, I'da' voted for one," Winthrop said.

The governor cocked her head and smiled in an enigmatic manner that Bea had noticed before in similar confrontations. "My dear sir, certainly you see your civic duty in this instance? Beatrice has been through unimaginable suffering through no fault of her own, and we should all try and make restitution. . . ."

"Bull!" Winthrop snorted. "My civic duty is to build a mess of condos for rich old people with plenty of jack."

"I think the emissions sticker on your pickup is out of date," Rocco said as he pulled a summons book from his back pocket.

"You don't bother me a bit, Herbert."

"Too little tread on the rear tires also," Rocco continued as he wrote.

"Everyone off my land!"

"Impeding an investigation," Rocco added.

"I'm calling my lawyers."

"What I don't understand is why you'd want to live in Nutmeg Hill," Kim said. "You just don't seem the type."

"I told you, the house goes." Burt Winthrop looked up at the house with a glance of disgust. "Damn place is an antique. I got a twenty-five-year-old new wife who likes nothing but modern. A few days from now, you guys can play pick-up sticks with what's left."

"Of course you'll have to live here," the governor said.

"The house can't possibly be torn down," Kim said.

"I bought this place and the deed is on file with the town clerk."

"That may well be," the governor said. "But this house and the rest of the property cannot be changed in any manner until the suit is settled."

"What suit?"

"Indians," Kim said breathlessly.

The governor smiled at Kim. "That is why Ms. Ward

and I are together this morning. We are touring the areas that the tribe is claiming."

"I'm with the Indians," Kim said. "Part one myself."

"Something about burial grounds on the property," the governor said.

"Oh yes," Kim added. "Burial mounds all over the place. You must warn your people not to disturb them, Mr. Winthrop."

"As a matter of fact, there are a bunch of Indian mounds on the property," Lyon said. "I had nearly forgotten about them."

"All right, you people," Winthrop raged. "I know a put-up job when I see it. You're all out to get me and I'm not going to sit still for it."

"The court injunction will be served this afternoon," Kim said. "Unless you want to deed this property voluntarily to the Indians?"

"It will probably be tied up in litigation for years," Rocco said.

"I got lawyers that can bust anything," Winthrop said. "Old Traxis has got a piece of this action, and he isn't going to stand for it either."

"Then there's the question of the Historical Commission," the governor said. "Kim Ward is on that committee also."

Kim smiled at Winthrop. "As a state historical preserve, the house cannot be altered without permission of the committee."

Burt Winthrop looked from one determined face to another and slowly sank into a wicker chair. "If it's not Indians and history, it will be something else. Always something else."

"'Fraid so," Kim said.

"I know when it's time to lick wounds." Winthrop shook his head.

The governor, Kim, and Bea walked back to the waiting

VW. "I hope you get your house back, Beatrice. I mean, where else would we hold our fund-raisers in the Murphysville area?"

Bea smiled. "Thanks, Ruth."

"How far back should I back-date the historical preserve?" Kim whispered.

"Make it two years," the governor replied. "We wouldn't want this to look like Watergate."

When Bea and Kim walked back to the patio, Rocco was sitting on the wall, smiling. Lyon and Burt were arguing over the interest to be paid on the money to repurchase the house.

"Same as commercial credit, Wentworth. In today's market, let's say 18 percent."

"That's robbery," Lyon sputtered.

"We'll pay prime rate," Bea said firmly.

The phone rang inside the house, and Rocco went through the French door to answer it. He returned a moment later. "The airport's on the phone, Lyon. They want to know how long you're going to keep the airplane."

"What airplane?"

"The guy just said a little one."

Lyon bolted for the house. "Oh my God! I've misplaced an airplane."

"Listen, Lady . . ." Burt Winthrop looked at Bea a long moment and then sagged. "Okay, I know when I'm beat. Prime rate plus four."